Sycamore Whispers

Shane Ledyard

Self-Published by Shane Ledyard

First Paperback Edition: November 1, 2017

Ledyard, Shane, 1976-

Sycamore Whispers: a novella / by Shane Ledyard-1st edition

Summary: Sweet Emma Sterling has lost her way after her beloved father returns home from military duty acting like someone she has never even met. Her once perfect life spirals out of control as her heart cannot bear the change in her daddy. Her mother's faith and a rogue horse with a troubled past may be Emma's only chance to get her life back to the way it once was.

ISBN-13: 978-06929462244 (Paperback)

ISBN-10: 0692946241

For my father, Dick Ledyard, who taught me how to love by my actions rather than words. Thank you for working so hard to give me a magical place to grow up and call 'home' forever.

CONTENTS

"But ask the animals, and they will teach you, or the birds in the sky, and they will tell you; or speak to the earth, and it will teach you, or let the fish in the sea inform you." ~ Job 12:7-8 (NIV)

Chapter One

The Sterling House

The creaking of a porch swing awoke Emma Sterling. Her eyelids flashed open to reveal the perfectly blue eyes of the ten-year-old. So blue and so perfect, they soaked in the sunlight that was shining in through the windows of her vintage Victorian home. A surge of energy shot through her body that elicited a playful squeal from the sweet girl as she whipped herself carelessly out of bed. She ran hastily down the wooden staircase and pushed open the screen door to find her mother swaying on the porch swing that had woken her from her sleep.

"Emma girl!" exclaimed her mother, Julia, just before the wooden door slapped the frame of the gray and white one-hundred-year-old home.

"Morning Momma!" Emma replied blissfully, bracing the porch swing awkwardly to give her mother a morning kiss.

Emma rubbed the sleep from her eyes as a pair of red-breasted robins flew to the porch railing. Dozens of other birds flooded the background with a kaleidoscope of tweets and busy chirping.

"Momma, why do these silly birds always come around you?"

Julia smiled at her happy, energetic daughter and then pulled her close for a proper hug that flooded the wooded-clad porch with love.

"I don't know, Emma. I suppose they like me. Or maybe they like listening to the swinging of the porch swing. Or perhaps, they just like to see you and your messy hair come running out of the house!"

Emma giggled and pushed herself abruptly away from her mother as she jumped to her next thought.

"Where is Daddy?"

As the words left her mouth, several more birds flew to the porch railing, cocking their heads as if they eagerly awaited the answer themselves.

"He went out early to get the morning paper. Even though it has been a few months, Daddy is still in army mode, so he was up before all of us, and he needed something to keep himself busy."

"I know what he can do to stay busy!" Emma exclaimed with enthusiasm, sending the audience of birds into a flurry across the yard.

"What is that?" Julia asked, knowing exactly what Emma was going to say.

"He can take me to the barn!"

Her mother flashed a doubtful look at Emma.

"Oh! Please Mommy; say it's okay with you. I really want him to take me to the barn. I haven't spent time with him all week, and I want him to meet the new pony. Please, Mommy…"

Julia rolled her eyes and acquiesced with an affectionate smile. "Okay, okay. I know you won't let up until you get an answer. But seriously, let's see what your father has planned for the day."

Emma had a button nose, plump lips, and dove-shaped cheekbones that cradled her blue eyes. The light sprinkling of freckles on her nose and cheeks were the only thing that kept her from being an exact replica of her mother. Emma turned quickly with a smile and ran back into the house to get a cold drink of water. Once she left, even more birds came back near Julia, anxiously moving their tiny feet along the porch railing, making the tiniest of sounds that you would hear only if the rest of the world had stopped moving.

Julia smiled as she thought of how proud she was of her daughter. Along with her naturally

3

delightful way, she was always eager to help around the house. At school, she had a reputation for including everyone interested in a playground game, and volunteered to help her teachers whenever there was an opportunity. She had become sympathetic to children that appeared to be left out; she knew the feeling well since she had already moved three times since she was born. Chase's position in the army forced the moves, although their latest destination, they hoped, would be their last.

Julia squinted as the summer sun gained strength, peering through the oak and ash trees that lined the south edge of the property. It was going to be a sultry, gorgeous day, and she planned on enjoying every moment.

Julia, Chase, and Emma had moved into Julia's childhood home just outside the small, charming Victorian village of Wycombe, Pennsylvania two years prior. The house had the intricate accents typical of a Victorian style home, and sat stoically atop a hill on two acres of perfectly manicured lawn. The rectangular property included a large, wooden barn, several gardens full of flowers, and a huge willow tree that sat just off center of the lot. It was a climbing tree with a colossal trunk that grew sideways for several feet before branching off upward with enough substance to form four other trees. When she was just a young girl, Julia would run to the

4

big tree if something made her sad, curling up just at the base of it, waiting for her sorrow to pass. As a teenager, she would steal away with her diary to the same place, hiding under the natural veil of the long, abundant branches of the willow.

Cornfields surrounded two sides of the property that stretched towards the forests. In peak season, the tall, green stalks gave Julia a wonderful, secure sense of knowing her boundaries and this made her feel quite content. Come winter, with the corn cut and the other crops turned underground, the brown earth lay bare, leaving no sense of promise, forcing the eye to look for hope far across the open field to a forest of maples, oaks, and random clusters of pines. In the center of the distant forest was a tremendous sycamore tree with electric-white and silver branches that stood out against the background of the plain, brown trees that had been stripped of their summer life. The tree had an alluring air about it that commanded Julia's attention as a child. It looked as though it stood waiting for her to come sit beneath its long, thick, powerful branches so it could tell her something that she needed to know, but due to her youth, was not quite ready to understand. Its presence comforted her and scared her all at once, so she stayed far from it, choosing only to look at it from time to time with the deep sense of awe that only children are capable of.

The nature that closely surrounded the home was especially appealing to Julia. There were mourning doves that would wake her in the morning with their quiet coos, and the owls would occasionally come to visit late at night. In the deepest parts of summer, just as the fire flies would start to blink wildly across the yard, she would watch as bats would fly in and out of the belfry of the old farmhouse from across the street. Somehow, she even adored the creepy, black bats that dove wickedly for peaceful prey through the dusk sky. Julia would lose herself in those summer time memories. She would recall running wildly up and down the rows of corn with her siblings and neighbor friends, chasing each other until they would tumble back into the yard with joyous exhaustion that caused them to laugh until their bellies hurt. These scenes of her youth replayed in front of her as she watched Emma. She loved these moments in her life, and a sweet warmth would wash over her each time they unfolded. Nothing, though, did Julia Sterling love as much as her darling daughter Emma, and her devoted husband, Chase.

A woman with clarity and reasoning, she managed to finish her nursing degree while raising Emma. She endured the challenge of Chase's career path in the army pulling him away for prolonged periods of time. She knew his life was frequently in danger, so she instinctively stayed busy to keep herself as distracted as she could. As with other army wives, there was always a part of her that worried about what the next day could bring.

As for Emma, she had horses to keep her busy when her father was away. She started riding when she was eight years old, just after they moved back to Julia's family home in Wycombe. Like her mother, she preferred having a set routine, which the horses certainly gave her. Also, quite like her mother, she did not realize how much she needed that routine to keep her mind off missing her daddy. She just did it because it felt right to her, and with it, everything always fell perfectly into place.

Chapter 2

Give Me Your Eyes

Chase's pick-up truck pulled into the gravel driveway and stopped abruptly. He leaned over the bench seat of the single cab, and opened the passenger door to let his border collie, Duke, run free. The wiry dog scrambled franticly out of the truck and ran straight towards Emma. He wiggled his body wildly; releasing his black, white, and brown hair into the humid, summer air. He peered up adoringly at Emma before running circles around her in the hope that she would play with him. Too intent on her own plans, she bent down and got a kiss from her excited friend, and then quickly focused her attention on her daddy.

Chase shared a broad, white smile that brought a glow to his pale blue eyes. He had dimples that stayed cheerfully in place even when he wasn't smiling, which left certain proof of his kind, affable way. A man of preparation, his muscular, lean, six foot-two-inch body was always in excellent physical condition. His standard off-duty dress was blue jeans and cowboy boots, topped with a clean, white, V-necked t-shirt. Despite his imposing physical presence, he was very mild-mannered.

"Daddy!" Emma yelped as she ran towards him, leaping trustingly into his arms.

"Emma girl!" Chase replied, opening his arms as she came charging towards him. He grabbed her around the waist with one arm and twirled her around three times, before placing a dizzy, giggling version of his daughter in front of him.

"And what are you doing today, Emma girl?"

"It's Saturday. Can we *please* go to Ms. Natalie's barn today?"

She batted her eyelashes coyly, gaining every last bit of her father's attention.

"Hmmm. I don't know," he replied in a teasing tone.

"Daddy, *please!*" she stared at him beseechingly; secretly knowing he had every intention of doing what she had hoped.

Chase flashed a smile. "Of course, Emma girl. What else would we do on this beautiful day?"

"Oh yay! Thank you, Daddy!" she screeched as she ran back inside the old house, followed closely by a joy-filled collie.

Julia got to her feet to give her husband a kiss. "Good morning so far?" Julia asked as she pulled softly back from Chase's embrace.

"Yes, so far so great."

She looked warmly at him, but sensed apprehension as he looked away.

"What is it?"

"We need to talk later," Chase replied softly, stealing the perfection of Julia's morning.

Julia's heart sank into her stomach. She knew exactly what the talk was going to be about; she just had not expected it to come so soon. He had just returned from a tour a few months prior, and she was hoping he would, at least, be staying the rest of the summer.

Chase took her wrists and gave her his broad smile until she reluctantly looked at him. The tears that had welled up in her eyes waited for her cheeks to get sufficiently red before sliding cautiously down.

"Hey now, everything is going to be all right. This will probably be one of the last times that I need to go away."

Before she could respond, Emma came back out of the house, with Duke following close behind. "Are you ready, Daddy? Ms. Natalie said we could come whenever we wanted to today. I

11

get to stay after my lesson and help out with the barn chores too!"

"Yes, Emma girl, sure thing," Chase responded, pulling Julia closer to hide her tears from Emma. "I will be right there, honey."

"We'll talk later," Chase whispered softly to Julia in an encouraging tone, searching her eyes with his. He wanted so badly to reassure her in that moment, but he knew she would need time to process the notion that he would be leaving them again so soon.

Julia nodded quickly and looked away, wiping her tears once more from her face, which was now blotchy and damp. Chase turned to walk to his truck where Emma was already in the passenger side, waiting eagerly for her driver.

"Come on Daddy, it's getting hot in this old truck!"

Chase climbed in with Emma and gave her another smile as they pulled out of the driveway past Duke, who had already found his place for the day on the cool, moist soil underneath the porch. They drove through the countryside to the barn, Emma with her hand out the window, shifting it side to side and fighting against the strong, pure breeze that pushed past the truck. Her brown hair blew wildly in the wind, sometimes covering her face altogether. She would push her hair back in a vain effort to get it out of her eyes. It didn't bother Emma, though. She never thought once to complain of anything. To her naïve mind, every little girl got to drive to the barn with their daddy, the windows down and making a mess of their hair. A certain sweetness from Emma's essence poured itself from the truck and into the green fields that they drove past. It was impossible to tell if the leaves on the wise, deep-rooted trees on the side of the road were blowing from the breeze, or if they were clapping for the chance to catch sight of the young girl who was so full of life and virtue.

The mood shifted as they neared the driveway of the barn. Emma was so excited, thinking about riding her pony, that she didn't notice the tension steadily building in her father. He knew he had to tell her that he was going away again, and it was even more difficult for him to tell Emma than her mother. She never cried or made him feel guilty when he gave her news of this sort; but guilt consumed him nevertheless. He was concerned that somehow, one day, he may responsible for her losing her wonderful spirit. This notion plagued his conscience. He valued Emma's innocence more than anything in the world.

Turning into the long driveway at Hound Hollow Farm, stones kicked up violently against the underside of the truck, startling Emma. She pulled her hand back inside the cab and rested it on her lap. The noise of the small rocks pelting the undercarriage of the truck continued until Chase brought it to a stop about halfway up the driveway. He strategically placed them by a hedgerow so they could benefit from the shade that the trees provided. He put the truck in park, took off his seatbelt, and turned with a thoughtful look towards Emma.

"Emma girl, there is something I need to tell you."

Emma still looked as though she was somewhere deep in her own world, so Chase used a phrase that he used since she was a toddler to get her attention.

"Emma girl, give me your eyes." Emma turned toward her father and focused on him. The humidity seeped into the truck despite the shade of the trees, and Emma finally started to sense her dad's forlorn mood.

"What is it, Daddy?" she asked, trying to hold onto the blissful state that filled her just moments before.

"Honey, Daddy is going to be going away for a while; the army needs me again."

He braced for her response.

"Can I come with you?" she replied playfully, cocking her head to the side with her hands on her cheeks.

"No, sweetie," Chase felt his mouth slip into a smile at her antics, but quickly forced it down to return to the seriousness of the matter. Their eyes both shifted outside as they noticed several turkey vultures circling over the field next to them.

"A deer must have gotten hit by a car," Chase whispered in a sad voice, just before giving Emma a tap on the leg to get her attention back.

"Emma, this time I may be gone for quite a while. But I promise I will get back just as soon as I am able."

"When are you leaving, Daddy?"

This time, her tone was more suited to the topic of conversation.

"Next month, honey. Next month," Chase answered flatly, forgetting to lift his voice to a reassuring tone.

Emma looked away, towards the barn, and nodded her head briskly. "Okay, Daddy. It's getting hot sitting here. Can we go down to the barn?"

"Yeah, sure." Chase replied. "Everything is going to be all right, Emma girl."

"I know Daddy, just like Momma always says, it is all going to work out. And one day you will come home and never have to leave us again."

"That's right, Emma girl. That's right."

Chase looked away from her and put his truck in drive. The turkey vultures had landed, seven in total, jockeying for position around the young deer that lay motionless in the field. One of the vultures glanced up from his meal as the truck started back down the driveway. It stared directly at Chase as he drove by, giving him an uneasy feeling. He wondered why such a thing would have bothered him at all, but the image of the bird staring at him while standing over the lifeless fawn lingered in his mind. Once stopped, Emma slipped quietly out of the truck while Chase grabbed her riding gear from the truck bed. He followed her into the barn, and after Emma gave him a tour of the horses, her instructor, Natalie Furlong, greeted him.

Natalie met them with a smile, but judiciously avoided small talk. A slender woman in her sixties, Natalie had been responsible for training the area's best riders over the previous three decades. She was a brisk and efficient teacher with a commanding presence that would sometimes override the natural beauty of the longstanding horsewoman. Her cerulean eyes would pierce through her company, but offered no judgment, even though it always felt as though the judgment was impending. It was a privilege to bring your child to her farm; if you did not appreciate it, you were weeded out with expediency.

Natalie bent over, placed both her hands on her knees, and looked straight at her student with a heartening smile. "You go find Cadence, Emma. She will help you get your pony ready. You will be riding Stormy today."

Emma knew not to run in the barn, but she was so excited to ride the new pony. In lieu of a full out run, she skipped to find Cadence. The stern horsewoman could not bring herself to correct her, as it seemed a sin to quell the raw joy of the young Emma Sterling.

"Thank you, Ms. Natalie," Chase said to her as she walked away to continue with her barn chores. "If it is okay with you, I will watch her lesson, and come back to pick up her up around four o'clock?"

"Yes, that'll be fine. Cadence will look after her and keep her busy. Emma does well helping with the chores. She certainly is a delight to have in the barn."

"That is great to hear. Thanks again, Ms. Natalie."

After Emma's lesson, Chase left the barn and drove home. On the way, he savored the breeze as it washed over him, along with the smell of summer filling his lungs. He thought of his adoring wife at home, and found himself in a boy-like state, eager to return to her for their Saturday together. While away on duty, he always regained a sense of appreciation for everything in his life. Even though being away from Julia and Emma caused his heart such pain; in a backward way, he appreciated the hurt, because he knew it made him acutely aware of the preciousness of each moment of his life.

His mother's rosary, swinging gracefully from the rearview mirror, came to rest as he parked in the driveway. Duke peered out from underneath the front porch but did not make an effort to get on his feet this time. The heat had sapped his motivation, and he lay prone, his sides heaving as he peered with glazed-over eyes at his master. Julia was just finishing watering her flowers, and the tears that were on her face when Chase had left were replaced with a sweat that caused her lightly tanned skin to glisten in the sun. Her hair was pulled up in a bun, with some strands trailing loose that framed her face, as her husband looked upon her with tender adoration. She graciously wiped a line of sweat from above her lips as she came to her feet. Chase came to her and kissed her; both their mouths slightly parted and their eyes closing just long enough to be in the darkness together for a moment. They smiled sweetly at one another, and Julia took her husband by the hand and led him to the porch.

They sat down at a small, round table that had been handed down from Chase's grandfather. The surface was full of scratches from decades of wear that Chase and Julia had promised each other they would never remove or complain about. The imperfections served as reminders of the trials and triumphs that their family had gone through. Chase reached across the oak table to take Julia's hand. She knew what was coming and looked away towards the cornfields that were standing virtually motionless in the stifling heat. She quickly pulled her hand away from his before he could say anything and blurted out the only diversion she could think of.

"Do you want some iced tea? I made some this morning."

Chase nodded, and a look of empathy came across his face.

Julia was doing everything she could to hold on to the perfection of the day. There were the red-breasted robins that stood curiously on the railing when she drank her morning coffee. The sweet aroma of the corn fields as the morning breeze whisked playfully across the porch. The sound of Emma rushing fervently down the steps to get her morning hug. And the sight of her husband, who she so dearly loved, coupled in hope with the thought he would never leave her side again.

She worked her way cautiously back to the porch with a glass of tea in each hand. She nearly lost her grip as she used her back to push her way through the screen door that Emma had burst joyfully through earlier in the day, sending the birds in a flurry out towards the willow tree. Gaining her composure to look Chase in the eye, she sat down in her chair, but found him gazing across the street at the old run-down farmhouse that looked as though it should be full of ghosts. She could see her strong, courageous husband was fighting tears. Sitting down beside him, she rubbed his hand gently. They sat silently together in the stillness of the summer heat, the condensation on the glasses running blindly down to the old table, leaving their own permanent mark. This time though, despite everything being so quiet, the robins did not bother to come back.

Chapter 3

Ophelia

On the surface, Ophelia was raised in a wealthy, privileged situation that most girls would envy. Much like where Emma Sterling lived, the grass was lush and the air smelled sweet, and animals of all sorts overtook the morning silence with a chorus of chirps, tweets, and pleasurable chatter.

The day she was born, there was a rare kind of aroma that filled the chilly, spring air with a blissful palatability. The air was a different kind of cool, much like when you pass through a small, mysterious patch of cold air on a warm, summer evening. Somehow, an atmosphere like this, when tied to a moment, can overwhelm someone, and sometimes bring him or her to inexplicable, joy-filled tears. This phenomenon, as it were, can even happen to a horse. This is how Ophelia started her life, but this extraordinary perfection would only last as long as her first few breaths.

Ophelia's mother, Temperance, seemed to hate her the moment she saw her. She stood looking away from her new-born foal, her ears pinned back, reluctantly waiting for her to nurse. As Ophelia made her first struggle to her feet and wobbled instinctively to her mother's side, the old broodmare stared blankly as her baby latched on for her first drink. Although Ophelia was filled with love for her mother, the chestnut filly with big doe eyes and a tender heart felt nothing of the sort in return. A nicker from a mare to her foal should be filled with love, but every nicker that she got from her mother was filled with disdain and disgust.

This was certainly an odd way for a foal to be treated by her own mother. Nevertheless, the relationship continued like this for the first several months of Ophelia's life. She always wanted to be close to her mom, but the opportunity rarely presented itself. Temperance was a big chestnut-colored Hanoverian-bred mare, with four white socks, and shiny dapples that showed up every summer on her hindquarters. Despite her beauty, she was a grumpy, nasty mare and she barely ever said anything to the young Ophelia. If she did speak to her, it was always in a discouraging, critical tone. Every day, Ophelia would watch the other babies play with their mothers, and she would hear the kind, positive things they would say to their foals. At first, it delighted her to hear her friends get praise. She was happy for them, as she saw how joyful and confident they became with each sweet word from their mother. The mares would give soft nickers of correction and praise to their babies as they taught them right from wrong. Ophelia could sense that these words were filled with love, and the other foals would seem to glow when they heard these affirmations from their mothers. Sometimes at night, Ophelia dreamt that her mother would talk to her like that as well. She imagined her mother nudging her along steadily with her nose, encouraging her to be brave when they encountered different terrain in the pasture. She pictured her teaching her about the frightening sounds they would hear at night. The call of a coyote, the screeching of a fox, or a spooked whitetail deer that would hiss and dash off through the woods at an unfamiliar smell. Instead, she would learn all this just by watching. She had to do her best to keep up, and was left to figure most things out on her own. Just once, she wanted to feel what the other foals felt when they were praised and reassured by their mothers, but she started to worry she would never feel that way herself.

Unfortunately for Ophelia, she was right. Over the next few months of her life, the lack of her mother's attention would break her tender, innocent spirit. The sadness eventually turned to bitterness, and then the bitterness led to an angry disposition. Ophelia was not a young horse filled with enthusiasm and promise. She was a sad, miserable, resentful wretch of a horse, and she was only five months old.

On a summer morning after dawn had broken, the dew burned quickly off the grass at the presence of the sun. Large, green flies awoke from their slumber and began to furiously bite through the thin flesh of the horses. Some of the bites were so sharp that little droplets of blood were left resting on their hair. Young Ophelia's short tail did not do her much service; so she stood close to her mother in order to fend off the wicked little parasites that were interrupting their morning graze. Temperance's tail swept through the droplets of blood, spreading it across her coat in streaks, creating the appearance that something far worse had happened to her besides the bite of a hungry fly. They were engrossed with the process of trying to eat while keeping their enemies away, when a terrifying scream from across the farm commanded their attention. She couldn't see what was happening, but Ophelia sensed something was terribly wrong. She had never heard another horse scream in such horrid despair, and she was sick with certainty that a coyote had come out of the woods to attack one of her friends.

"Mother, why is he so upset? What is happening?"

"Never mind Ophelia, just mind your own business."

"But Mother," Ophelia replied. "Shouldn't we do something? It sounds like he is in trouble."

"That's going to be happening a lot in the coming weeks, so you better just get used to it," the old mare replied callously.

"Why, what do you mean?"

Ophelia was becoming quite afraid, and her voice quivered as she spoke.

"Exactly how it sounds. Every foal needs to be weaned from his or her mother at some point. He was born before you, so he goes first."

"Goes…goes where?"

"Away."

"What do you mean, 'away'?"

"I don't know. Stop asking so many stupid questions. Can't you see for yourself? You are on a breeding farm, Ophelia. The owners made you so they can sell you. You are money to them; that is what all of us are. Money. Every foal that I have ever had has been taken from me and I never saw any of them again. I suppose they think you are going to go be some big show horse. With your crooked legs and narrow chest, I wouldn't expect you to get very far though. You just better hope you get a home and don't end up in a kill pen."

"What is a kill pen Mother? Why are you telling me these terrible things?" Ophelia's voice cracked as a tear welled in her eye, causing the once crisp vision of her mother to blur.

"Never mind, Ophelia. Just go back to grazing."

"But," Ophelia stammered worriedly.

Before she could say another word, her mother pinned her ears back and bared her teeth at her daughter, a clear signal to stop asking questions. Temperance did not want to hear another word about it; she put her head down to eat the grass, as the terrified screams of the colt being weaned from his mother echoed across the farm.

All the horses on the farm were unsettled, but they were soon brought into the stable for the hottest part of the day. That afternoon, Ophelia noticed her mother acting differently than normal. Her head was down and she had stopped eating. She would occasionally bite at her sides, as if something was bothering her belly. Ophelia went over to her, and noticed that for the first time she was not just in a bitter mood, but she actually looked despairing.

Ophelia looked up at her mother, unsure of what to say to her. She swallowed hard, and with an innocent, tender voice inquired, "What is the matter, Mother?"

"Nothing Ophelia," replied the old mare, not bothering to turn her head.

Ophelia persisted, "I can tell something is wrong; you aren't eating and you keep biting at your sides. Does something hurt?"

"Never mind, I said. Just go back to your hay," the old mare retorted, this time with a mild pinning of her ears.

Unfortunately, none of the barn workers noticed that Temperance wasn't herself that evening when it was time for them to be turned back out. The barn girl that led her out to the pasture was too preoccupied with her evening plans; she didn't bother to follow proper turnout procedure. She hadn't noticed that Temperance left her evening meal of grain untouched, and she should have stayed to watch the mare trot out to her field and put her head down to graze. Instead, she turned away, not aware that Temperance took just a few steps, stretched her neck out and snorted at the ground instead of diving into the grass as she normally would.

Ophelia was starting to get truly concerned and persisted with her inquiries, determined to find out what was the matter. She offered a tender nicker. "Momma, please…please tell me. What is wrong?"

The old mare softened quite a bit when she heard her daughter call her "momma". She took a deep breath and turned to her in a mothering posture that Ophelia had never seen from her before. It made Ophelia uncomfortable and warm all in the same moment. She braced for her mother's reply.

"It is the weaning, Ophelia; I don't like the weaning. I don't like seeing the sadness and fear in the foals when they are taken from their mothers."

"Doesn't that have to happen? We all get weaned, don't we? I heard the other foals say that we are destined to do important things and we are here to help people. We have to get weaned to make that happen."

"Yes, Ophelia, I know why foals get weaned, and I…" she stopped mid-sentence to bite her side once more. Her compromised state left her emotional, and the tough old mare offered somewhat of an apology to Ophelia.

"You need to understand something Ophelia. I have been on this farm nearly my entire life. You are the seventh baby that I have had, and that will make you the seventh foal that I will never see again. Once you are weaned, that's it. Forever. The first foal I had; her name was Madeline, and I loved her so very much. When she was taken from me I was devastated, and my heart was never the same again. I know the other mares think it is their job and their lot in life to produce horses for people to enjoy, but I can't get past the hurt of losing everyone I love only months after they are born."

Ophelia looked down and away. She was starting to feel guilty that she had begun to resent her own mother. She understood at once why she had been acting the way she had. She only wished that she had known all of this from the start. She looked up as her mother started to paw the ground, another sign that she was more than just upset about the weaning; she was in pain.

"What is it, Momma?"

"Nothing, Ophelia; probably just too much rich grass after the rain. I will be fine."

The old mare knew better, though. She knew that something was wrong, but none of the barn workers would be back to check on them until morning. She knew she was starting to colic, and that she needed help from a human. Her stomach was starting to hurt terribly, but she instinctively did her best not to show any signs of panic for Ophelia's sake.

The next morning, the barn manager was the first person to arrive to the barn. She saw Temperance was in distress and called the vet straight away, starting the barn protocol for colic. Ophelia heard them say that they were going to have to wean her from her mother at once. She wasn't sure what was happening, but she noticed one of the younger barn girls trying to hold back tears. She looked worriedly to her mother, and the mare dropped her head in an invitation for Ophelia to come closer to her. She wrapped her neck gently over top of her last foal, and gave Ophelia a tender nicker. And for the very first time, the nicker was filled with love.

Chapter 4

Pig of a Horse

The air that had been so sweet when Ophelia was born still washed over her every spring, but she never recognized it as anything special. Whatever hope and kindness she had in her heart left her when her mother died, leaving behind a sullen, common, little wench of a horse. A horse such as her would have normally been taken to an auction or sold cheaply to the first available dealer, but the trainers and the owners at the farm took pity on her. They sent her to the barn's auxiliary training facility; about seven miles south of the breeding farm, shortly after her mother passed and she spent the next three years of her life there. The trainers at the barn nicknamed her Orphan Ophelia, and assigned her to the working students who were just learning how to train horses. This way she wouldn't take up the time of the top trainers, but she still served a purpose to the business.

They found she was quite easy to saddle break and train, but everything she did was colored by the poor attitude she had adopted as a foal. Because she was born with mediocre conformation and a common look, the farm's head trainer and manager was eventually forced to sell Ophelia to keep costs down. The barn was a quality operation that did right by the horses; they took the time to devise a plan for each horse they thought would best suit their potential. Other horses at the farm would one day be sold for tens of thousands of dollars, but not Ophelia. Her crooked legs, narrow chest, and lackluster demeanor would limit the height she could jump, thereby reducing her potential to fetch a large price on the open market.

It took some time, but Ophelia was eventually sold to a teenage girl in Pennsylvania, named Lydia. Lydia was a natural rider with patience and persistence that allowed her to make the best of what she had with Ophelia. She was a kind girl, with olive skin, almond-shaped brown eyes, and a pleasant, but rare smile. She had long, slender legs that she wrapped firmly, but sympathetically, around Ophelia's rib cage, giving the horse no reason to do anything but cooperate with her. She had strong arms for a girl her age that tapered to soft, sympathetic hands that gently guided Ophelia through the jump courses at her first several horse shows. The ornery mare was fortunate to have such a girl ride her at the beginning of her career, but didn't show any real signs of appreciation in return. She followed orders well, but her lack of enthusiasm discouraged Lydia, who wanted desperately for the mare to show more of a spark and interest in her work.

"What is the matter with you, girl?" Why do you always seem so angry?" Lydia asked her one day after she had gotten done working her in the ring.

Ophelia wished she could respond, but she just stared blankly past Lydia. She was so depressed that everything hurt, and when the young girl talked about her dreams as a rider, it just made Ophelia feel worse because she knew she could never live up to her expectations. She sensed that her time with Lydia was ending. A visit later in the week from Lydia's trainer, Karen, confirmed her suspicions.

Lydia kept Ophelia at home, so Karen would come to her property to give her lessons. Karen came early to the barn this day and arrived just as Lydia was tacking up. As Lydia tightened the girth, Ophelia pinned her ears and shook her head

33

angrily side to side. It was close enough to Karen that she thought the mean look was directed at her.

"She is *such* a pig of a horse, Lydia. Why don't you just get rid of her?" Karen asked, giving the mare a nasty look.

"Oh, she is not that bad, Karen. She has always been good to me, even though she is a bit of a grump."

Karen was not impressed with Lydia's response. She never appreciated Ophelia, and ever since she started working with Lydia, she had worked to figure out a way to get her to sell her mare. A tall, skinny girl in her late twenties with a spray-tan, bleach-blonde hair, and tiny brown eyes that were too small for her face; she carried with her an inferiority complex that colored everything she encountered. She was just pretty enough to be approachable, and knew *just* enough about horses and horse-showing to sell her below average services to unsuspecting parents and teens.

"She has been a nice tool for you to learn the ropes with, but if you want to move up, you are going to have to move on from her."

"What are you thinking, Karen?"

"You are too talented for her, Lydia. You can do so much better. You should talk to your parents and see if they would consider getting you something else."

Ophelia pinned her ears back, but this time her angst was undoubtedly in the direction of Karen.

Karen countered the threatening look from Ophelia with venom in her voice. "She is such a nasty little mare!"

Lydia bit her lip. She was offended, but didn't want to outwardly disrespect her trainer so she kept on with tacking up.

"I know she is not the sweetest thing in the world, but I have good memories with her."

"Memories, Lydia, memories." Karen's beady eyes emulated a false empathy for the impressionable Lydia. "If you want to accomplish your riding goals you are going to have to do better than 'memories'. You need a horse with a better attitude that can jump the bigger jumps. Just picture what you could be doing. I know you like her, but this mare is never going to get you to the top. You really need to talk with your parents."

Ophelia could tell what Karen was doing. She could also sense Lydia starting to cave. She started to panic, and shifted herself nervously back and forth in the crossties in the aisle way. She tried desperately to warn the naïve Lydia. She flicked her nose up and down, and pawed the ground to get her attention. Karen had enough of Ophelia's nervous behavior and screamed in her face.

"Knock it off!"

She stepped in front of Lydia and snatched Ophelia's halter hard, causing her to jump back. "You stupid…"

Before she could finish her sentence, Ophelia reared in panic and broke the cross ties. The ceiling in the barn was low, and the top of her head struck it, tearing the flesh between her ears. Blood seeped down between her eyes, while her steel shoes scraped the concrete floor in a clamor. Frightened and rejected, she fled desperately to her stall, scraping the saddle on the doorframe as she went in.

"Stupid! Stupid pig of a horse!" Karen lamented, standing indignantly as Lydia walked calmly towards Ophelia's stall to get the situation under control. She looked in and found Ophelia frightened and panting furiously, her eyes wide in terror.

The following month, they took Ophelia to a local horse show where she turned in another mediocre performance. Karen sensed an opportunity; she could tell Lydia's dad, Richard, was getting frustrated with the results. She tried to appeal to his competitive side to motivate him; she knew he was a businessman who only thought in terms of winning and losing.

"Having a horse like Ophelia is liking bringing a Volkswagen to a NASCAR race; you might be able to go around the track, but you are never going to win. There are a lot of horses out there that could help Lydia accomplish her goals. Ophelia just isn't that horse. I don't need to tell you, Richard; *you* know what it takes to succeed."

"I get it, just find Lydia what she needs to win. I am tired of getting beat. It's embarrassing. I don't need all the details, just make it happen."

"No problem," she replied, her beady eyes narrowing as she tried to hold back a smile. She already had the replacement horse lined up, and she had it arranged so that she was going to make a lot of money on the commission. She did everything but salivate at his response.

"I don't want to be feeding a horse that she doesn't need, though. What are we going to do with Ophelia?"

"She really is such a tough horse to sell. She is so common, and the people I know just don't have any interest."

Richard shot her an aggravated look. She quickly came up with a plan to keep him happy and in the buying mindset.

"Actually, I have been thinking a lot about this for you. I think I know exactly what you should do with her. There is a barn down in Bucks County that handles horses just like her and should be able to get her sold for you."

"Where are you talking about?"

"You should send her to Natalie Furlong. She needs to go to Hound Hollow."

Chapter 5

Daddy's Home

The night before her father was scheduled to come home, Emma could not fall asleep. Julia went in to check on her before she went to bed and found her daughter under a sheet with a small flashlight, putting on a play with two of her favorite stuffed animals. Through the muted light glowing through the pink sheet, a puffy gray squirrel and a fat raccoon worked out Emma's secret thoughts. Julia did not dare interrupt, so she stood quietly in the doorway, discreetly listening in as Emma brought her nighttime friends to life.

"What are you so worried about, Squirrel?" inquired the plump raccoon. Emma had given the stuffed raccoon the voice of a man, and Julia did her best to keep herself from laughing aloud at the impression. She covered her mouth with her hand, and listened as the play continued.

"My daddy has gone away to collect nuts and I haven't seen him in a long time." The squirrel replied in a melancholy tone of a worried little girl.

"When will he be coming back?" The raccoon wanted to know, his voice deeper than before.

"He will actually be back tomorrow," the squirrel's voice continuing to emanate a hopelessness that the raccoon could not ignore.

"So, why do you sound so sad?" he pursued.

Julia shifted her weight at the doorway. Her amusement turned to concern at the direction of the dialogue. She noticed that the shadows on the wall looked more like wicked monsters than the small, stuffed animals that were actually under the sheets.

This time, the fictitious voice of the squirrel was gone, and it was replaced with the trembling sob of a little girl. "Because I am afraid that when he comes back, he won't remember who I am."

Julia shifted her weight again, this time causing the wood floor to creak beneath her feet. Emma heard her and popped her head out from under the sheet. The squirrel and the raccoon resumed their lifeless state, and Julia slowly approached the bed.

"Hey Emma girl, what are you doing still awake?"

"Nothing Momma. I just can't sleep."

"Is there anything you want to talk about?"

"No, I'm okay," Emma replied, shifting over to make room for her mom to sit down next to her.

Julia stayed and gently stroked her daughter's hair until she fell asleep. Emma fell into a deep sleep and dreamt of her daddy coming home, picking her up, and twirling her around like he always did. In her dream, he stopped her mid-twirl and locked eyes with her before bringing her slender, youthful body to a halt in front of his sturdy frame. He would quickly pick her up again, and she would giggle and screech as they tried to hold eye contact while he twirled her. The dream went on, and she saw flashes of herself doing all the things she loved to do with her father. She dreamt in vivid, living color and smiled as she slept.

Julia awoke well before dawn and went to Emma's bedroom to check on her. She gazed tenderly at her sleeping daughter's serene face as it soaked in the milky-white moonlight from the window.

She took a deep breath of air that saturated her presence at the doorway with peace. Her thoughts turned to the fact that Chase was coming home. Her family would be complete again, with all the pieces of her life in place, as she thought they should be. She slipped back through the hallway to her bedroom, and curled up in her bed. Clutching a pillow tightly, she prayed for her husband's safe arrival. The moonlight poured through her window too, but it did not drench her face with tranquility as it did Emma's. The large ash tree outside created a fractious image through her window that left thousands of tiny shadows whipping back and forth across her face. A storm crept up from the east, sending the spring leaves into a furious state. Despite the long branches of the old ash scraping anxiously against the siding, Julia fell asleep.

Later that morning, a light breeze cleansed the air and pushed the storm clouds gently towards the west, leaving behind a blue sky dotted with large, puffy, happy clouds that made shapes that could mean different things to different people, depending on how they saw the world. Emma and Julia held hands and swung on the porch swing, waiting for Chase to arrive. The creaking sound of the swing was at a quick pitch, as Emma's excitement generated a strong push from her legs.

With every car that passed, Emma looked on with anticipation. The morning wore on, and just as she started to become discouraged, a cab pulled into the driveway. She bounded gleefully off the porch to her father, with Duke following closely behind, his tail wagging fervently. Chase bent down to hug his exuberant daughter, but there was no twirl-through-the-air given, and he barely made a sound as he brought her close to his chest. His normally hearty hug was mechanical and almost cold. Meanwhile, Duke had stirred himself into a chaotic frenzy and came to rest at Chase's feet and rolled over for a belly rub, but the belly rub he was hoping for never came, and he just lay there, questioning why he had bounded off the porch to begin with.

"What is the matter, Daddy?" Emma inquired immediately. This was not even close to the reaction she had envisioned and dreamt about. Julia quickly answered for her weary husband as she took his right hand in hers.

"Oh, Daddy is just exhausted, Emma. It was a long trip."

Chase mustered a smile for his wife and wiped a tear from her cheek as he gave her a hug, his camouflage bags still clutched in his left hand.

"Hi, honey. I missed you." His normally broad, warm smile had been replaced with a half-smile that elicited little emotion.

"Oh God, I missed you too! I missed you *so* much! I am so happy you are home safe," she whispered in his ear. She took the bags from him, put them down in the driveway, and tightly wrapped her arms around his back while resting her head against his chest.

Chase stood stiffly and barely reciprocated the affection. Julia sensed something was off and took a step back from him, while keeping one arm around his waist.

"Hey, *really*, are you okay?"

"Yes, I am fine. Like you said, I am just extremely tired. I think I will go in and lay down for a bit."

Emma broke the quiet moment with her youthful enthusiasm, hoping it would perk her father up.

"Daddy! Do you want to go to the barn today?"

"Emma no!" Julia corrected sharply, "Daddy has been traveling for hours; just let him be."

Chase looked toward his daughter. "Maybe we will go tomorrow, Emma. Maybe tomorrow."

"Yes! Thank you, Daddy; I want you to meet all the new horses at Miss Natalie's. I have so much to show you!"

"Emma, please." Julia warned her daughter.

"It's okay, Julia, she's just excited. I will get some sleep and we'll all talk later, okay?"

"Yes, of course," she whispered intently, with concern dominating her face.

Chase took his bags and walked inside. The last bit of joyfulness of his return left the moment the screen door shut behind him as he went into the house alone.

"What is wrong with Daddy, Momma?"

"Oh, honey, he just had a really long day. He'll get some rest and he will be the daddy you know again tomorrow."

The next day came, and things did not get better; nothing changed the day after that, either. Months passed in the Sterling home, and Chase did not "become himself" again, as Julia had promised. He actually went the opposite direction, and became more withdrawn from both of them, as well as everything else in his life. He took a job as a driver for a local nursery that sold plants, shrubbery, and trees to local landscapers. This position would enable him to be by himself for most of the day. He maintained a routine every week that was designed to keep him isolated from the rest of the world. He went to work each morning, returned home for supper, then went straight to bed. He exchanged pleasantries with the people around him, but only said enough so that no one would consider him rude.

Both Julia and Emma could tell something was not right, but neither of them knew how to communicate it. When either of them would touch on any of the topics beneath the surface of common conversation, he would become irritable and sometimes even snap at them. He was not the man that Julia had married, and he was certainly not the father that Emma had known. The most they could get from him was a small smile when Emma would come into the room for her evening hug and kiss good night. Even this small, tender moment seemed like a chore for this once loving and caring man who had been so full of life.

After weeks of the same peculiar behavior, Julia started reaching out to her friends who had husbands that served in the military, trying to gain insight. She had to be careful though, as Chase's position in the army was something that he valued immensely. His father and grandfather served in the army as well, and Chase was very proud of the family's military legacy. If she poked around too much, she was afraid she would damage his marquee reputation. She struggled to find answers. It was too difficult to describe his condition without too many questions being asked. She chose, instead, to stay silent and hope that he would get back to being himself on his own.

As the months went by in the old Victorian house where the once perfect and lovely Sterling family lived, the situation with Chase had not improved. Despite the prayers and the tenderness of Julia's presence, nothing seemed to make a difference. Emma had grown tired of trying her childish tactics to cheer up her father, and instead reduced herself to being polite to her dad.

Julia surmised from her research and her talks with close friends that Chase was suffering from post-traumatic stress disorder. The horrifying things he had witnessed in battle had taken a toll on his mind. Worse yet, for Julia, was the fact that it had also had a brutal effect on his heart. The condition that afflicted him came with a host of other issues, and he had lost interest in all the wonderful things that had given him pleasure before. His emotional detachment was likely a subconscious way of protecting Emma and Julia; creating a paradox that was destroying their relationships. He knew his actions were causing the suffering in his family, and the guilt he experienced was crippling. He did not know how to bring it to light and change what was happening. He was in such a terrible depression that he felt like someone was standing on his chest and not letting him breathe or move, so making a substantial change in his life seemed impossible. He wanted so much for things to go back to the way they were, but his mind and his body were somehow stopping him, making him blind to any opportunity to take control. It was like he was living inside a terrible dream, where everything around him was being destroyed, and he was powerless to change it.

Julia refused to give up on what once was her amazing, lovely, and perfect life. She prayed constantly for strength and for Chase to heal. She needed answers, she needed a way, but there seemed to be nothing that was going to help or heal the love of her life.

And then there was Emma. On the verge of turning twelve, she was utterly lost; she was lost without her daddy and lost without her mother's attention, which was now focused solely on the mission of helping her husband. Every day she would walk off the porch that was once filled with love, leaving the chirping birds, and the reassuring creak of the porch swing behind her to face the world on her own. The innocence, the joy, and the happiness were fading away; and so was the sweet Emma Sterling.

Chapter 6

Emma Girl Gone

Fall arrived without warning; cutting the summer heat sharply with a cold breeze that forced people into flannel shirts and sweaters before the calendar bothered to turn to October. Emma had fallen into the habit of storming out of the house to go to the bus stop without saying a word to either of her parents, with the exception a mumbled "good-bye." The screen door that slammed behind the solemn daughter used to be a sound of unity in the Sterling house. Now, it just served to break a looming silence that was colored with anger and frustration.

Her school and social life had also diminished. Concerned teachers kept Julia informed of her daughter's decline. The girls that used to come by for play dates stopped coming by. Much like her father, she had an instinctual urge to separate herself from the rest of the world. The loss of her relationship with her dad was too much for her young heart and mind to bear, so she turned inward, as far away as she could get from the person she once was. Julia never thought that Emma would lose her passionate enthusiasm for life, especially at such a rate.

The weekly trips to and from Hound Hollow for Emma's lessons were reduced to a form of torture for Julia. Emma would stare out the window of the car, her lips pursed together tensely, pre-loaded with a venomous reply should her mother dare speak. The change in Emma's personality hurt Julia in a different way than Chase's transmutation; she could not get through the air of hate and bitterness that surrounded her. The car rides that used to be filled with laughter, childish giggles, and secret mother-daughter chats were replaced with a palatable negativity that superseded all the delight they used to enjoy. Julia would confide in her friends about Emma's change, but the advice she received was always the same. They blamed hormones and said that she was just a "typical pre-teen." Deep down, though, Julia believed she knew better. She knew better, because she knew her daughter's true heart; she *knew* this was not who her "Emma girl" was meant to be.

Once at the barn, the routine continued with Emma exiting the car with an inaudible good-bye. Despite the rejection, and no matter how coarse the treatment, Julia would wish Emma a nice ride on her horse and tell her that she loved her. Some days the car door would slam shut before she could even finish her sentence. On days like this, Julia would get half way up the long stone driveway of the farm and stop the car under the same hedgerow where Chase and Emma watched the vultures. She would sit quietly by herself for a few moments, and then, as if it were involuntary, she put her head in her hands and sob until there were no tears left.

This same routine went on for weeks, until one day, instead of letting Emma get out of the car, Julia grabbed her arm to stop her.

"Emma, what is happening to you?"

"Nothing, I am fine. I have to go. Let go of me."

Julia pursued, "Emma, I can tell you are hurting. Please, honey I want to help."

"I am fine, Mom, really. I should go; I need to be on time for my lesson."

The normally cool Julia lost control. "Emma, please! You don't talk to me anymore; I need to know what is going on. You have changed so much!"

Emma tried to pull away, but Julia wouldn't let her. She turned and screamed in her mother's face, blind from the anger that she had bottled up inside.

"Fine! It's Daddy! It's Daddy!" Emma shrieked repeatedly. Tears poured down her cheeks that had become red hot with rage and hurt.

"He hates me! He won't even look at me!"

Julia tried desperately to cut her off.

"Oh, honey, your daddy doesn't hate you. He just…"

Emma wiped at the tears on her face in a fast, haphazard fashion and growled vehemently, "I asked him to give me his eyes, like we used to do, and he wouldn't. He just stared straight ahead! He hates me, he hates me!"

Emma pulled away from her mother's grasp and got out of the car. She slammed the door and stomped to the barn without looking back.

Julia started to tremble. She put the car in drive and stopped half way up the long driveway at the hedgerow. This time, though, instead of crying, she chose to pray. The windows of her sedan were partially open, allowing the cold November air to seep in and down the back of her neck. The silver cross necklace that draped her neck caught the light of the setting sun, sending fragments of light dancing across the dashboard of the car. She could smell leaves burning in the distance, and looked solemnly out at the bare trees that looked as though they would never see life again. A flood of consciousness came over her, and her thoughts wandered back to the summer that Chase had left to do his last tour. She stepped cautiously through every memory that led up to the present moment. Then she focused to create a vision in her mind's eye for the future. She struggled at first, seeing nothing but strife and malice in her life. Every time a terrible vision would come, she would chase it away, fervently praying and believing for her life of joy and happiness. The terrible images would come back, and she would chase them away as fast as she could, praying harder and with more passion every time the evil thoughts would start to overwhelm her. She started to believe for peace in her home. She saw visions of holding Chase's hand, and them joking together in the gardens at the house. She smiled as she saw Emma running down the stairs in the summer to give her a morning kiss. She envisioned the strong embrace of Chase around her slender body, and felt his hand gently caressing her cheek.

Again, the negativity would strike, and she would fight it off. She prayed harder. Tears of joy and victory were now streaming from her hopeful eyes. She closed them tightly and smiled warmly as she envisioned Chase twirling an older version of Emma around, their eyes locked on one another. Suddenly, she opened her eyes and brought herself back to the present moment. She felt a sense of peace pour into her body. She thanked God for every wonderful thing she had ever had in her life. She wiped her tears and set off for home, leaving the smell of the burning leaves and the barren trees behind her.

When she pulled in her driveway, she took a long, deep breath. It was starting to get dark, but as she got out of the car, she looked across the desolate field and saw the deep-rooted, white sycamore she used to stare at in awe as a child. The stark branches stretched out from the massive trunk against the distant, dark forest. She paused and gazed at the tree that had watched her grow up from afar. She soaked in the sight of it, brilliant in all its wisdom, as it seemed to comfort her and lend her fresh courage. She shook her gaze and walked towards the Victorian home that was completely dark, apart from a soft glow coming from her and Chase's bedroom.

She knew she had to talk to Chase about how their lives had changed so dramatically since he came back from military duty, but had been reluctant to confront him. He had been so out of sorts that she did not want to upset him or make his condition worse by saying the wrong thing. She knew that she had to say something, though. If she continued to be silent, she sensed things would only get worse for all of them. She prayed for the right words as she made her way through the living room and up the creaky, wooden staircase towards the bedroom.

"Chase, are you here?"

No response.

"Chase!" She hollered, and hurried nervously up the steps towards the bedroom.

"Chase!"

"I'm in here," he replied in a faint voice.

She pushed open the bedroom door and found him sitting by the window in a rocking chair with their wedding album in his lap. The lace curtains draped in the window moved eerily as the breeze from the hastily opened door washed across the room.

"What are you up to honey? You scared me when you didn't answer."

I - I just..." He struggled to find words. "I just wanted to look through this. It's been a while."

She knelt down next to him and looked on as he slowly turned the pages of their album. He paused when he came to a candid picture of them dancing together. His arm was just above her waist, and she was leaning back and laughing, with a genuine smile full of joy. Their look of adoration for one another was unmistakable, eliciting a pure, heavenly glow.

Julia broke their attention from the picture as she took Chase's arm gently.

"What is happening to us Chase? What is happening with you? You haven't been the same since you came back. Not even close. I am so worried about you."

"It is nothing I can talk about. I will be fine." Chase stared at the floor, refusing to meet her eyes.

"You keep saying that, but nothing is changing. You are not fine. I am not fine. Emma is not fine. What happened with Emma this morning, Chase?"

"Nothing."

Chase stared out the window with no expression on his face. Julia persisted.

"She is not acting like it was nothing. Chase, what happened? What is happening?"

"Nothing! Now please go!" He screamed abruptly, causing Julia to recoil towards the door.

Julia wasn't used to Chase, or any other man she knew, raising his voice at her. She started shaking, but began to pray again.

"Stay strong and courageous. Stay strong and courageous," she repeated in her mind.

She wanted to lash out at him, but instead, she spoke tenderly; it was the tone she used the first time she told Chase that she loved him. It was the same voice that she used when Chase lost friends in the war, and when he lost his parents in his early twenties. She leaned down to him, cupping his face gently and stared intently into his eyes. He tried to look away but she pulled him back each time he tried to avert her gaze. Drawing out each word, slowly and clearly, she asked him once more. "What happened, Chase?"

His eyes burned into hers as he screamed, "She asked me to give her my eyes! She asked me to give her my eyes and I couldn't! I could not do it!"

He screamed so loud that the wood floor beneath him shook. Julia did not react with anger; she instead looked deeper into his eyes. "So, that is your special thing with your daughter, Chase. She just wants to connect with…"

He cut her off.

"I couldn't do it! I can't do it! I'm a monster! Can't you see that? I am a *monster*!"

Julia stepped back. "I don't understand. You are not a monster; I love you! *We* love you! I don't understand how you…"

"Nobody gets it! Nobody understands! You don't know what I saw. You don't know what I went through! You don't know what I had to do!

"I *want* to understand," Julia interrupted, trying to show him just how much she loved him. "You were protecting our country. You are a hero, Chase. Don't you get that? We love you no matter what happened over there. And whatever happened is all in the past. We are right here in front of you. *This* is now. I just don't understand how…"

Chase just looked away. "You will never be able to understand. Never!"

Julia started to lose her composure. "We can't go on like this, Chase. You need help," she said vehemently. "Perhaps I cannot help you, but somebody can! Please Chase!"

Chase just looked away and fixed his eyes on the window. This was the look he would give when he would completely disconnect. Disheartened and emotionally exhausted, she turned to walk away. Just as she was about to give up on the moment, she noticed a slight change in his posture. She moved back to his side and put her hand on his shoulder. Using what seemed like all of his strength, he lifted his arm and pointed at a picture that Emma had painted on her seventh birthday. She was so proud of it, so they had it framed and hung it on the wall. It was a watercolor portrait of a chestnut-colored horse. The picture was flawed in many ways, typical of what you would expect from a young child. The bridle, which should have gone behind the horse's ears was only halfway on, with the brow band resting awkwardly just above the horse's eye. The shape of the head was asymmetrical, with one nostril quite larger than the other. The horse had a long mouth that curved upward at the edges and led up to large, strong cheekbones that gave the horse a look of strength and peace. The eyes were large, and colored a deep black, and they would follow you around the room wherever you walked. There was something special about them - something promising and beautiful.

As he pointed, a tear dripped down his cheek and fell to the ground.

"That picture. That is what I feel like. I feel like I have been made wrong. I feel like I am broken."

Tears were now pouring from him as he came back to the present moment. He turned to Julia, fell from his chair, sunk to his knees, and collapsed into her arms. He wept like a child as she held him. Despite all the sadness and despair, she could not help but feel hopeful. For the first time since he had returned home, Julia was able to embrace her husband.

"We can work through this Chase, everything is going to be all right," she reassured him as she rocked him gently back and forth. She paused for a moment and pulled away slightly. She cupped his face again, and locked eyes with him. "*Promise me* that you will get help."

"I will, I promise," he repeated, "I promise."

With a voice saturated with love and concern, he turned back to the subject of his daughter.

"Oh my God, but what about Emma? What about our sweet Emma? I feel like I have destroyed her. I don't know what to do for her."

Julia held his hands tightly, and held fast to his gaze. "I want you to focus on yourself for now. I have a plan for Emma. I believe I know exactly what will bring her back."

"Okay, okay," he agreed as he lifted his chin level to the ground and nodded his head yes.

An energy full of promise surged through Julia's body, starting deep in her belly and welling up into her heart. For a moment, she felt like the woman she once was. The wonderful memories of her life with her husband and daughter came flooding back into her consciousness and brought her to her feet. She could see the woman she wanted to be in her mind with absolute clarity. She was the mother who sat on the porch swing on the pure summer mornings, waiting to see her daughter so she could start her day with encouraging words. She was the one for whom the robins flew to the porch rail; watching prayerfully over her and her family and giving her a sense of peace. She was the one with faith and expectancy, and she was the one with a heart that always believed that everything in the world works together for the greater good.

Chapter 7

Mean Girls

The next day, Julia drove directly from work at the hospital to Hound Hollow Farm to see Natalie Furlong. She had worked the night shift, and the combination of sleeplessness and the torrent of emotions from the day before left her in a strange state of mind. As she got closer to the barn, she began to feel anxious, despite being so sure of herself the day before. As soon as she turned into the driveway, she felt unease curl around her stomach, as she watched the fog lift from the field, as the rising sun burned the morning frost from the dead, cold November grass. She hastily passed the hedgerow where she had been stopping to cry. From there, she drove on cautiously, the gravel tenaciously pelting her car. She considered turning back, but just as a plan to retreat formed in her mind, the fog cleared enough for her to gain view of a single, dark bay horse trotting anxiously up and down the fence line. The horse was trotting thirty yards, skidding to a stop, then whipping its body back the other direction to a slow gallop, stopping fast again before turning back to repeat the process. The horse's anxious manner was contagious, and she started to feel overly warm, queasy, and unsettled. She chewed her lower lip worriedly, and brought her car to a stop when she saw Natalie come out of the barn with another horse. It was a plain, chestnut-colored horse that walked steadily beside her, and it did not bother to look up as it went by. She waved timidly to Natalie when she saw her, convinced she had made a mistake showing up at the barn unannounced. She was afraid that Natalie was not going to agree with her plan, and her lack of sleep was compromising her sense of reason. In that moment, she recognized that the Devil had flooded her with fear. She took a deep breath as she squeezed the cross around her neck tightly in her right hand. Her mind cleared, and she pushed herself past the doubt that had seized her.

She parked the car and met Natalie, who was walking back to the barn, now empty-handed. Julia could see in the distance that the dark horse that was pacing the fence had settled in. Natalie had turned the chestnut mare she was handling out with the bay for company; when they connected, the two horses touched noses briefly and trotted off to the middle of the field to graze. Julia felt a chill as she saw steam billow from their large nostrils towards the earth and float back to their faces, clouding their vision.

Natalie greeted her with a smile and went directly to concern for the exhausted-looking mother.

"Good morning, Julia. I certainly didn't expect to see you this early in the morning. Is everything all right?"

"Yes, everything is fine... Well, perhaps it isn't. I just…" She tripped over her words. "I just needed to run something past you," she stammered. "Is now a good time? Should I come back?"

"As long as you don't mind talking while I work, now is as good a time as any," Natalie kept moving as she motioned with an encouraging look that put Julia at ease. They continued back down the drive to the barn so Natalie could go on with her morning chores.

"So, what would you like to talk about?"

"It is Emma. She, well…" She sighed and started over. "I think we should get her a horse."

Natalie stopped mid-step and focused all her attention to Julia.

"You have been around here enough to know how much work and money is involved with horse owning Julia, so I will save you that speech. But what makes you think your daughter needs a horse?"

"I don't want to burden you with details of our home life, but things have been difficult recently. Emma is really struggling, and…"

Natalie interrupted. "I have noticed the change in Emma. She used to be so bright and bubbly; she does not say much anymore. We *love* having her here, she just isn't the Emma we used to know."

"Does she ever talk to you about anything?" Julia inquired hesitantly, unsure that she even wanted the answer to her own question.

"No, no. She keeps to herself. She goes right to the horses when she gets here, and she doesn't say a word when she takes her lesson. When it is over, she goes right back into the barn. I have no complaints. She is just really quiet, and it is so much different than how she used to be."

"Well, she will be turning twelve next spring, and I…"

Natalie interrupted her again, and this time abruptly. "Age has *nothing* to do with why someone should own a horse; I am sure you have a better reason."

Julia could feel herself getting emotional. She did not want to dump everything on Natalie, but she started to let loose anyway. She talked without taking a breath, and Natalie listened patiently as Julia confided everything. She started with the summer day that Chase told them he was leaving for another military tour, and ended with the trip to the barn that morning. Natalie listened without judgment as Julia went in and out of emotional control, her flood of words finally slowing to a trickle and then stopping entirely.

She took a deep breath, paused, and looked Natalie straight in the eye. "I am losing my little girl. I don't know why, but I believe in the deepest part of my heart that a horse will somehow save her."

Natalie nodded sympathetically as she put a reassuring hand on Julia's shoulder.

"Okay. Let's take a walk."

After delegating the morning barn duties to Cadence, Natalie took Julia back up to the field that they had passed earlier. She pointed out across the pasture at a chestnut mare that stood grazing alone.

"That mare there, she would likely suit Emma well."

Julia was not expecting Natalie to show her a horse straight away, and it caught her off guard.

"Really? She is beautiful. Has Emma ridden her before? What is her name?"

The questions came faster than answers. Natalie motioned with her hands for Julia to slow down. "Her name is Ophelia. And no, Emma hasn't ridden her yet. She came in a few months back on consignment. She was a tough little mare when we first got her, but Cadence and a couple of the other more experienced riders have done well with her. She has come a long way in a short while."

"What is her story? Is she expensive?"

"No, no. She is well within anyone's budget. The sellers just want to be rid of her. The child that owned her has moved on to another horse with more ability."

"I don't mean to question you Natalie, but why do you think she would be good for Emma even though she hasn't ridden her yet?

"Just a gut instinct, I suppose. She is a horse that needs her own person. I think a girl in Emma's situation could use someone or something they can help. This horse will be a challenge, but she will be safe, and Emma will be able to handle her."

"You have always done right by us. Just tell me what we need to do from here and I will make it happen."

Julia did as she had promised and followed Natalie's lead. Within two weeks, Emma Sterling became the owner of the plain, crook-legged, chestnut mare named Ophelia. The day Julia walked in the barn and introduced Emma to her, she just stood and stared in disbelief.

"Really Momma? She's mine?"

Ophelia lifted her head up from her hay and stared at Emma, wondering why she was so excited to own her.

"Yes, Emma, she is all yours."

Emma turned and hugged her mother and then ran to Natalie and embraced her as well.

"I don't understand. Why did you...?" Emma was so ecstatic she had trouble forming words.

"Good question," Ophelia thought, "What would they want with me?"

"We all thought you were ready, honey," Julia said to Emma, trying to hold back her tears.

"Can I groom her, Ms. Natalie?"

"Yes, of course, Emma. Like your mom said, she is all yours."

"Thank you, Ms. Natalie!"

She quickly turned to her mother.

"Wait, does Dad know?"

"Yes, honey. He knows."

"Okay, good. I am going to groom *my* horse now," Emma said, her voice trailing off in a tone of wondering disbelief.

She carefully walked into the stall, and Ophelia turned toward her so that Emma could put the halter over her head. She attached the lead rope, and walked Ophelia out of the stall to the aisle where she clipped her to the cross ties. Ophelia was not enthused like Emma, but she stood quietly as her new owner groomed and made a fuss over her. She started with her mane, combing it over to the right side until it laid flat against her neck. She then carefully combed her forelock, making sure not to pull any of the hair out, and laid it gently back down on the mare's face. Then she took a currycomb and curried her hair in a circular motion to loosen the dust, and followed with a hard brush to whisk away the dander that had appeared. She followed with a white rag that she rubbed vigorously over her, bringing her chestnut coat to a brilliant shine. Ophelia was agreeable as Emma picked the dirt from all four of her feet, and then Emma surprised her with a mint from her pocket. She nodded her head in appreciation after the sweetness from the red and white striped candy spread across her tongue. Natalie had gone back to her chores, but Julia sat on a tack trunk across the aisle, and looked on in delight at what she was witnessing.

That night in her stall, Ophelia wondered why anyone would want to own her. She remembered everything that Karen had said about her; she knew she had crooked legs and was nothing special, because even her mother had told her that. She thought about how she had come to be at Hound Hollow, and pondered what her life was going to be like with Emma as her owner. She thought how getting attached was not an option for her. She assumed that Emma would soon tire of her and move on to a more talented horse, or even lose interest in horses altogether. As the night wore on, she listened to all the happy horses at Hound Hollow contently chew their hay, and it nearly hypnotized her. She fell into a half dream-state and let her mind indulge in the idea that Emma really did like her and accepted her for who she was. *Maybe, just maybe,* she thought to herself, *I really am worth something. Otherwise, why would this girl Emma be so excited to own me?*

This idea pleased her and warmed her heart; a feeling she wasn't at all used to. A slight chill seeped into the two-hundred-year-old bank barn, but the thoughts that she had about Emma stayed with her, and kept her mind off the change in temperature. Her eye lids fluttered as she fell into sleep, but was awakened shortly thereafter by a furry, gray mouse about the size of a walnut, that slipped through a crack in the worn, wooden boards of her stall. She heard it let out a high-pitched squeak and snorted loudly at the sight of the tiny creature as it darted towards the remnants of the grain from her dinner. It glanced up at her in a flash and smiled a cunning smile out of the corner of its mouth just before he grabbed his snack and scurried off anonymously into the night. The commotion broke the stillness in the barn and the other horses in the aisle all lifted their heads from their hay to look at her.

Across the aisle, a black and white paint pony that had been lying down scrambled to her feet at the disturbance. Her name was Pansy. She was one of the older lesson ponies that many of the children had learned to trot on. Her base color was black, and she had white splotches that made wild shapes across her body. Whenever a new rider would meet her, they would try and find something in the pattern of her hair, such as a heart or stars. Everyone found different shapes when they looked at her. That was something she liked that about herself. It distracted people from a scar beneath her eye that she got trying to reach under a barbed wire fence for sweeter grass when she was a yearling, growing up in Texas. The wire tore her eyelid, making it appear she was always crying - but only out of one eye. She was a kind pony that always took care of her riders; her only vice was she could get very cranky if her sleep was disturbed. She was not pleased when Ophelia and her antics with the mouse woke her up.

"What is wrong? What is going on?" she yelled, her eyes wide as she ran circles in her stall. Hay and dust flew everywhere, causing her to snort and sneeze, adding to the ruckus.

"Nothing," replied Ophelia. "Nothing at all. Sorry I disturbed everyone; it was just a mouse."

"A mouse," Pansy hollered back. "I hate those! I never call them 'mice'. I just call them rats. All nasty little rats! They are worse than pigs."

When the she heard "pig", Ophelia's mind went back to the day in the barn when Karen had called her a "pig of a horse". With the memory came the feeling, and she sighed deeply as she thought to herself: *A pig of a horse. That's right. That is all I am, just a pig of a horse.*

Pansy stretched, yawned, and after a short while looked over and saw Ophelia staring blankly at the wall. She sensed something was not quite right with her stable mate.

"What is wrong with you, Ophelia? It was just a mouse."

"I know."

"Sure, and it's gone; so everything is okay. Why don't you go back to your hay and stop looking so sad? It was *just* a mouse."

"Right, I know Pansy," Ophelia sighed with palatable sadness, "and rats are even worse than pigs."

♦ ♦ ♦

Of course, Emma had always dreamt about owning a horse. In that dream, everything about the horse would be perfect. She had imagined, like any young girl may, that her horse and she would be best friends. They would gallop in wide, open fields and then Emma would lie on her neck and give her a big hug after each ride. She envisioned her bedroom wall would be full of ribbons and pictures from the competitions they would enter. The horse would nicker to her when she walked in the barn and she would give gentle kisses with her muzzle when Emma left her for the day. Something like that - that is what a little girl might imagine. The winter months that followed, however, fell far short from the image she had built up in her mind. Far short indeed.

She was agreeable about being groomed, but Ophelia brought her sullen attitude to every ride with Emma, which frustrated her terribly. When Emma would ask her to go forward, Ophelia would pin her ears and grind her teeth. As the other girls in the barn progressed steadily, Emma seemed to be going backwards with her training. When no one was watching, Emma would go to battle with her. She would saw the reins back and forth in an act of self-defeat, forcing the bit to rub hard against the corner of Ophelia's mouth. Ophelia would dig in against her efforts, so Emma would jab her in the ribs with her spurs in a desperate attempt to get the mare to cooperate. This was their relationship, and for whatever reason, no matter how much they struggled, neither of them could figure out a way to fix it.

As winter departed and spring attempted to welcome a now twelve-year-old Emma Sterling, the frustrations between them continued. On one windy April day, just past Easter, the two went to the ring for a hack; this time the mare was worse than usual. Emma became enraged with Ophelia and lost control of herself.

"You stupid horse! I can't stand you sometimes!" She ripped the reins upward, hitting the top of Ophelia's mouth. She then kicked her forward, raking her spurs on the mare's sides. Ophelia just slapped her ears harder against her head and rung her tail in a circle, balking at Emma's tantrum.

Emma was rabid with anger. Just as she was about to take a whip to Ophelia, she felt the presence of someone staring at her. She glanced over and saw Ms. Natalie standing at the side of the ring. Immediately, Emma was sick with embarrassment and shame. She braced for the tongue lashing that she so rightly deserved, but it didn't come. She looked down and away from Natalie, who just turned and walked into the barn, leaving an air of disappointment lingering around Emma and her uncooperative horse.

She wasn't sure what to do. She went ahead with her ride, and simply rode Ophelia's on a loose rein and settled for a simple ten-minute trot around the ring. Later in the barn, she was faced with a silent Ms. Natalie. Emma wanted desperately to say something, but she knew she was completely in the wrong and that there was no excuse for what she had done.

She looked up at her teacher shamefaced. "I am *so* sorry, Ms. Natalie."

"Don't say sorry to me, Emma. You need to apologize to your horse. That was quite the display you put on out there. What was that all about?"

"I…I just don't-" Emma stammered, fighting tears and the temptation to lose her temper again. "Why doesn't she listen to me? Is there something that I am doing wrong? Is there something wrong with my riding?"

"No, Emma. There is nothing wrong with the way you ride. You just haven't figured each other out yet. You need to give it time. Developing a relationship with a horse can take months, sometimes longer."

"I feel like I already have given it time," she replied, with an annoyed tone in her voice.

"Oh, Emma," Natalie replied, trying to hold back a smile. "Time with horses is different than our time. They think and respond differently than we do."

Emma stood staring back at Natalie with a discouraged look. Her shoulders were slumped and she looked as though she could cry at any moment.

"I wish they could talk."

"If they could talk, it would be too easy, wouldn't it? Horses are here to help us become a better version of ourselves. They are here to teach us. That said; they don't have a choice in the matter. They never asked to be ridden and they certainly should never be brought to task the way you did to your mare. You have to rise above the difficulties, Emma. It is up to you to figure out how to make the relationship work."

Emma nodded silently. Tears started to fall down her cheeks. She wanted to tell Natalie the truth. She wanted to tell her how mad she was that her dad was not coming to the barn to watch her ride. She wanted to tell her how she resented him for going from being her best friend to becoming emotionally absent. She wanted to tell her she was mad at God for letting this happen to her. She wanted someone to understand, someone to listen. She thought her horse was going to be her best friend and she thought she would start to feel the way she did when she was ten. She thought Ophelia might replace the feelings and friendship she had lost with her dad. She wanted to talk about all these things, but instead of being able to verbalize them, they just made her terribly angry.

Natalie's encouraging words got to Emma's heart, but they didn't give her ability to ride Ophelia well. She continued to battle her mare nearly every time she was in the tack, although it was more of a quiet struggle now, as they seemed to just tolerate each other. Emma did keep trying though, and every week she would show a small amount of improvement in her lessons. Things still did not seem to be coming along fast enough for her, but she did her best to take her trainer's advice and remain as patient as she could.

Then, just as spring turned to summer, a new boy and his horse came to Hound Hollow, and their arrival would change the way Emma looked at horses, and her world, forever.

Chapter 8

A Boy and His Horse

A teenage boy that rode horses at Hound Hollow was quite unusual. They pretended not to be interested, but Emma, along with the other girls, found this phenomenon most fascinating. They secretly studied everything that the boy did around the barn and with his horse. He was tall and thin, fourteen-years-old, with olive skin and black hair that peeked out in the form of curls from underneath his riding helmet. His brown eyes gleamed happily as he rode his horse harmoniously around the ring.

Emma had become very curious about him and had quietly managed to be riding in the ring the same time he was one day after school. She was far too shy to say hello to him, and she was taken aback when he trotted over to her in a carefree manner and greeted her without any hesitation.

"Hi. What's your name?"

Emma was immediately flustered and her face turned a bright red.

"It's Emma. Emma Sterling," she stuttered awkwardly.

"Nice to meet you. My name is Stephen and this is my horse Doc."

The boy spoke in quick, kind tones with an innocence that is typically long gone in a boy his age. He looked straight at Emma as he spoke, and emanated a gentleness toward her that made her comfortable, although she was still not sure what to say to him. She stared at the boy's horse and marveled at his condition. He was quite fit, with a dark bay-colored coat that was slick, like it oozed oil, causing it to shine in multiple patterns when the sun struck it. He had white socks on his front legs that stopped just below his knees, and a white marking on his forehead shaped like an upside-down heart. His horse stood calmly as Stephen went on speaking, his eyes half shut and his back leg cocked with his pastern resting on the ground, as though he had nothing in the world to worry about.

Emma did not realize it, but she had been staring at Stephen for quite a long time without saying anything. It startled her when he spoke again, this time with a smile that took up residence on just one side of his face. He accompanied it with a nod of his head that made Emma feel at ease.

"Your horse is pretty. I love a classic, plain chestnut horse. She looks like she is out of one of those old hunt prints that Ms. Natalie has in the barn. What is her name?"

"Ophelia."

"Ophelia? That means 'helper' doesn't it?"

"I don't know," Emma tripped over her words, "does it?"

"Yes, I think so. Anyway, she's beautiful."

"Thank you. Wait, how would you even know something like that, about her name?"

"My mom was Greek, so she was always telling me the meaning of different names."

"Oh, I see. Well, my horse is not much of a 'helper' to me. I don't even know if she likes me."

"What do you mean?"

"I mean she doesn't act like she likes me. Her ears are always back when I ride her and she sucks back when I put my leg on her to ask her to go. When she jumps a course, she goes really slow, and hardly tries to pick up her legs over the jumps."

"Oh, she seems nice to me though. I bet she likes you. Maybe she is just upset about something else that you don't even know about. She lets you get on her, that counts for something. She could just buck you off if she *really* didn't like you."

"Oh, I suppose you are right."

"Have you had her out on a trail ride yet?"

"No, I don't even know if she would go on a trail ride safely. There are so many things on a trail that I am afraid might scare her - like the deer and coyotes - or even a squirrel jumping out of a tree. Besides, I want her to be a show horse. I don't want her to get hurt."

"Just because she is a show horse doesn't mean she can't trail ride. Ms. Natalie seems to encourage it and some people say it makes a sour horse happy."

"Oh, I don't know," she searched for an excuse but could not find a good one. She really wanted to go, but was afraid Ophelia would behave poorly and embarrass her.

"No big deal," he relented, shrugging his shoulders. "Just let me know whenever you are up for it. It will be fun."

Emma did not have a chance to reply with anything but nodded eagerly as Stephen smiled broadly and went back to working with Doc.

It took a few weeks for Emma to get the courage to take Stephen up on his offer, but she finally worked up the nerve. After their Saturday barn chores were through, they tacked up their horses and set out on their ride. They made their way to the back of the farm where a narrow path led them through a large grove of pine trees. The scent of the pines drenched the air in the peaceful woods, putting them both in a pleasant mood straight away. At the end of the pine grove, they worked their way down a long, steep embankment laced with yellow and purple wild flowers that large, black and yellow bumblebees were tending to. Once back on level ground, they came to a farmer's field that had a long, worn tractor path. The path evenly split two fields that were full of new crops that seemed to smile as they peeked up through the rich, brown earth. One of the crops they could not identify, but Emma was certain the other was going to be sweet corn. Seeing the corn coming up reminded her of being on the porch with her parents and all the wonderful fun they used to have. In that moment, she saw in her mind's eye her mother's welcoming morning hug and her dad coming towards her to give her a big squeeze and ask about her day. She could see Duke panting in expectation of everyone's next move, wanting so much to play with them. Her entire sense of self overflowed with the wonderful feeling that the memory gave her, but in the next moment she became equally sad, as she realized that a memory was all it was. She shook herself back to the moment and stared straight ahead at the path in front of her.

They continued on, with Emma choosing to ride Ophelia cautiously behind Doc and Stephen. The tractor path was long, and with no cover from trees, the hot sun shone directly on them, lulling both the horses and their riders into a relaxed state. As Emma became more comfortable, she noticed something different about Ophelia. Her ears were forward, her stride length had increased, and her tail had stopped swishing every time Emma asked something of her; it was as though she was actually happy to be ridden.

Stephen took notice of the change in the mare as well. "She looks thrilled to be out here! Her ears are forward and everything."

"Yes, I noticed that too! I wonder what the difference is?"

"Maybe there is something out here that reminds her of a happy time in her life. Or maybe she is excited to see something new."

"Yes, maybe, I guess. Whatever it is, she certainly is nicer to ride when she acts this way."

"Who knows? But if she likes this, wait until she sees the stream we get to cross!"

"Stream?" Emma questioned, her voice high pitched with worry.

"Don't worry, Doc knows all about the water. He will show you the way."

For the first time in a very long time, Emma Sterling found herself happy. She followed Stephen and Doc as they turned right to go along a gravel road, which they followed about a half of a mile. Without warning Emma, Stephen turned Doc off the road and up a steep embankment that led to a sod field. Emma followed him up the embankment and squealed with laughter as Ophelia was almost vertical going up the steep hill. Her back legs pushed hard underneath her and she started to scramble as the soft, late spring soil gave way. The feeling was something that Emma had never felt, and it left her bubbling with giddiness as she slid to the back of her saddle. As they crested the hill, she righted herself in the tack. She was laughing so hard that it became infectious. Stephen began laughing too and the two of them acted as though they were ten years old again. They kept on laughing until tears came, which made them giggle even more. They were saturated in happiness and it was the most honest, vulnerable moment that Emma had experienced since the day her dad had stopped the truck under the hedgerow at Hound Hollow.

Stephen paused his laughter just long enough to make a suggestion.

"Do you want to try a gallop?"

"Sure!" Emma replied without hesitation, despite the fact she had never once galloped in her life.

The pair nudged their horses' sides with their heels while making a kissing sound with their lips to encourage Doc and Ophelia to take off. In moments, Ophelia went from a steady canter to a ferocious gallop. Emma set her hands on Ophelia's neck, clutching a mixture of mane and sweat-soaked leather reins. Ophelia grabbed at the ground with her hooves, madly pounding the earth beneath her. Emma had a fleeing moment of panic as she passed Stephen and Doc, but she had no intention of stopping the rush of freedom she felt. The wind caused tears to stream from her eyes and blur her vision as the sound of Doc and Ophelia's hooves battered the soft spring turf, sending dirt flying behind them with every step.

The woods were fast approaching, so Emma and Stephen pulled up on the reins and brought the horses to a walk. The horse's nostrils blew wildly and their sides heaved with urgency to retrieve their air. They steered their mounts through the woods and towards the stream, giggling and joking with one another like they were old friends.

Emma hesitated as she approached the water. The stream was quite wide and almost three and a half feet deep. The sight of it intimidated Emma and Ophelia knew it. They stopped at the edge of the stream and Ophelia spread her front legs while stretching her neck out to touch her nose to the water. Her eyes bulged wide and she quickly drew back to the safety of the stream's bank.

"You will be fine," Stephen encouraged, reading the look of uncertainty on Emma's face.

"Okay, why don't I follow you?" Emma suggested quietly. As brazen as she was at the gallop, she feared the water terribly. It was as if the water meant something to her - something significant, but she could not verbalize what it was.

"What are you afraid of, Emma?"

"I don't like that I can't see the bottom, and I am afraid something might happen to Ophelia."

"You will be okay. You have to trust her and let her know that you believe she can do it. Follow me and when you do, just squeeze her sides and keep your hands soft on the reins, so she has her neck to balance herself."

Doc waded in obediently for Stephen. Afraid to be left behind, Ophelia followed, her whole body coiled like a frightened cat. Emma was tense as well, but eased her hold on the reins as Stephen had instructed. Halfway through, Ophelia relaxed and took the last few steps out of the stream at a trot. Water splashed all over them and the childish laughter returned with the relief of getting safely to the other side. They stood together, the odor of the horse's sweat mixing with the stream water, creating a wonderful, rich smell unlike anything Emma had ever experienced.

The ride home was much more relaxed. The kids chatted easily about horses and nature. Stephen was quick to point out the different animals they saw along their way. He also liked to talk about the trees and how they grew. He pointed out how they seemingly grew with purpose, their branches going whatever direction they wished, giving shelter for animals and a place for tiny birds to land and rest their busy wings. He was an intelligent boy and he saw the good and the purpose in everything around him.

He certainly was interesting to Emma. He seemed far too young to know so much and it started to make her wonder how he had become the way that he was. She kept her thoughts to herself as they turned back down the gravel road. She guided Ophelia to a safe distance behind Stephen and Doc; about three horse lengths, as the horse's hooves struck the ground simultaneously, making a rhythmic sound that lulled them into a sense of refuge from the rest of the world. The breeze blew lightly, causing the manes on the horses to shift slightly, while drying out the sweat and stream water on the horse's coats, leaving patterns of a random nature, emulating the clouds that hovered quietly above them. The sound of the hooves relaxed them both, and with each passing step, a feeling of contentment settled into Emma's heart. The mood broke when Stephen casually mentioned a robin he saw land in a bush as they passed by it. With it, Emma began thinking again about her mother and the time they spent together on the porch when she was a little girl. She started to feel terribly guilty about the way she had been treating her. Stephen noticed her expression change.

"What's wrong Emma?' Why are you so sad all of the sudden?"

"Oh, nothing. Nothing at all."

"Are you sure?"

"Yes, I am sure," she wanted to change the subject before Stephen pressed on with more questions. She was not ready to talk with him about such things, as she was not even sure how to make sense of the things she felt.

"Can I ask you something though?" Emma asked, her facial expression and tone one of honest curiosity.

"Sure, what is it?"

Stephen slowed Doc so that they could ride side by side. Emma rode up beside him, the horse's footsteps now out of sync.

"What makes you so happy all the time? I mean…what I mean to say is, why do you always seem so happy?"

"Nothing *makes* me happy. I just *am* happy. My mom would always tell me it was my choice. 'Keep things simple', she said. 'Be kind to others, do what is right, and keep things simple.' She also told me there was never a good reason to worry about anything. She said that worry was the thief of joy. I do my best to follow what she taught me every day."

Emma tried politely to correct Stephen. "You mean teaches you, not taught, right?"

"No, I meant taught."

There was a pause. It seemed to Emma that it should have been a sad and reluctant pause, but it was not.

"My mom passed away when I was nine," he said in a soft and quiet voice that trailed off behind them as they made their way down their path together.

Emma struggled to find words to respond with. She had been so caught up in her own world and problems that she never noticed that his mother did not show up to the barn. She was horrified by her selfishness, and turned to apologize to him, but got the sense, looking at him, that she did not have to be sorry after all. When she looked at Stephen, she saw his beautiful, brown eyes, and to her amazement, they still looked as though they were smiling.

Chapter 9

Seem To Have A Song

That evening, Cadence and the other barn workers turned the horses out just before dark so they would be less likely to be pestered by the tiny, wicked black gnats that had taken up residence all over the farm. As the night overtook the daylight entirely, they would be replaced by thousands of fireflies blinking their miniature lights wildly across the pastures, marking the true arrival of summer in Bucks County. Doc and Ophelia were turned out in fields next to one another on the south side of the property. Both of their fields had rolling hills that led down to a steep valley that was covered in wild multi-flora rose bushes. In the center of the valley was a wide, cold stream with shifting white rapids that made a deep, comforting sound that joined the chorus of toads croaking fervently in the darkness. The stream bordered the farm, creating a natural boundary to the adjoining property of wheat fields. Between the stream and the fence line of the pasture grew a large grove of sycamore trees that were wide and tall, and had seen several generations of horses before Doc and Ophelia. Their patchy, white bark stood out against the deep, dark forest that dwelled behind them. Their branches reached in thousands of directions as if they were desperately grabbing for something that they deeply desired, while at the same time seeming deeply satisfied with their ability to provide shade for the horses and beauty for anyone or anything that thoughtfully paused to appreciate their splendor.

Exhausted after their long trail ride, Doc and Ophelia went to the bottom of their pastures to let the cool air coming up from the stream run over their backs. The sycamore trees stood stoically nearby, seeming to listen without judgment as the two new friends went over the highlights of their day.

"That was quite a ride, today, wasn't it?" Doc asked Ophelia.

"Yes, it was. That was the first time I ever crossed water like that. I loved the way it felt, especially when it splashed my belly!"

"It was also the first time you have seemed happy since I arrived at this barn. What makes you so grumpy all the time? Do you hurt somewhere?"

"No, not really. I just don't care to be happy or not happy. I just am."

"What about your rider, Emma, don't you want her to be happy?"

Ophelia gazed at Doc with a confused look. "Why should I care how she feels?"

"Because she is your person and that is your job. It is your purpose to protect and take care of her. The better your attitude, the easier it is for your person to enjoy you. Hasn't anyone ever taught you that?"

"No, not really. I mean I heard other horses talk about it, but I never really understood what they meant."

"Can't you see how badly she needs you? I do not even spend time with her and I can tell how badly she is hurting. She is such a sad young girl."

"You don't know what I have been through, Doc. My mother was awful to me when I was a foal. She told me that she thought everything she did was without a purpose. She didn't believe in any of these things you talk about. She kept me from the other foals and told me no one cared about me. She told me right before she died that the only thing people care about is the money. She told me…"

Doc cut her off mid-sentence. "That is your *mother*, Ophelia," Doc replied. "That is not you. How can *you* think you don't have a purpose?"

"I don't know…. I never really thought about it."

"Well you should think about it. Just look at the little girl who rides you. She is in so much pain and you can help change that. Everything has a purpose, Ophelia. Everything. I used to be miserable, just like you, until I found Stephen. He is so full of joy despite his circumstances. I think it would be a sin for me to do anything but be my best for him. Emma needs you and you have been placed in her life for a reason."

"What do you mean by 'placed' in her life?"

"Just look at everything around you, Ophelia. It all works together for good, if we allow it. Think about how the grass grows for us every year, how the trees give us shade, and the water comes from the sky and quenches our thirst."

As Doc spoke earnestly to Ophelia, the wind began to pick up and they turned together to look at the eastern sky for signs of a storm.

"Listen to the trees around us, Ophelia. Even as a storm is coming, the leaves of the sycamores seem to have a song. I think they may even be whispering something that we need to know. Everything, if we pay close enough attention, has a purpose. *Especially* you."

Chapter 10

Trust Her

Emma was anxious to get to the barn the day after the trail ride. She had a lesson scheduled with Natalie and she wanted to see if there was any difference in her mare as a result of her great ride the day before. When she left the car, she surprised Julia by being the first to say "goodbye," even offering a little smile as she quietly shut the door.

The moment she got in the tack, it was clear Ophelia was listening better to Emma. Natalie made mention of it and the usually quiet Emma started gushing with the tale of the trail ride with Stephen.

"Thank you, Ms. Natalie! Stephen took me on a trail ride and it was so much fun! We went through the stream and everything."

Natalie smiled and nodded quietly, affirming her approval before continuing the lesson. It continued to go well until it was time to jump. Emma was holding Ophelia back and not releasing her face over the fence, and it was frustrating Ophelia. Natalie sensed an opportunity to reach Emma in a way she had not been able to before.

"You have to let this mare be, Emma. She is a good horse, but the more you try and control her, the more she is going to resist you. You have to trust her."

Emma nodded her head in acknowledgement. Natalie instructed her to canter down to a jump that was higher and wider than anything they had ever attempted. Emma asked Ophelia to canter, and following Natalie's instructions, she softened her hands and gave the mare total freedom at the base of the obstacle. Ophelia exploded off the ground and jumped in a beautiful arc, landed softly on the other side, and cantered away from the jump gracefully. Her ears were pricked forward and there was tremendous joy in her canter step. Emma got goose bumps all up and down her arms, and as she pulled Ophelia up to a walk, she glanced over to see Natalie beaming proudly. Emma was elated and she reached down and hugged Ophelia tightly around her neck. The coarse hair from the mane pressed against Emma's cheeks as she squeezed Ophelia. She bit her lower lip to try and quell the tears of joy that were beginning to slide off her cheeks onto the common, chestnut-colored mare beneath her. The tears absorbed into Ophelia's soft coat as Emma turned her head to the sky with a grateful heart.

Ophelia could feel the love pouring out of Emma, and she stood proudly as Natalie and Emma heaped praise upon her.

"That was beautiful," Natalie complimented. "She was terrific. I think that is enough for your mare today. Now why don't you take her out for a bit of a walk down the tractor path?

"Really Ms. Natalie?" Emma could hardly contain her excitement. "By myself?"

"Yes, you'll be fine. Just go down to the end and turn around."

Emma and Ophelia headed out of the arena and down to the tractor path. Ophelia was a little more cautious by herself than when she had Doc to follow, but she did everything that Emma asked of her. When they got to the end where Natalie had instructed her to turn around, Emma felt the urge to go a little bit farther. She figured she would be okay since she was there yesterday, so she turned Ophelia up the stone road towards the embankment where the sod field was. It took longer than Emma thought, and when she reached the sod field she started to get nervous about her decision as storm clouds started to make their way towards them, covering the setting sun. She felt bad that she had disobeyed Natalie, so with her conscious getting the better of her, she turned to go back down the embankment. Just as she was pulling Ophelia's head around, two deer jumped out from some tall grass and spooked Ophelia. She jumped sideways and bolted, accidentally whipping Emma violently off her back, and onto the ground. Ophelia caught sight of Emma lying still in the grass and it caused her to panic. She took off at a full gallop to the barn.

Emma lay still on the ground; scared and shocked as her tender heart yearned to understand.

"Why?" she lamented, "why does this always happen? Why does everyone always leave me?" she questioned as she sobbed listlessly in between her quick and desperate breaths.

Ophelia stormed wildly down back down the road, heading for the tractor path. The stirrups bounced against her sides, which only added to her panic and confusion. Her instincts and self-preservation told her to go back to the herd where she would be safe. She galloped blindly back towards home, but as she neared the small rows of corn, she suddenly recalled Stephen and Emma being so happy there, and then remembered Doc's corrective words about how much Emma needed her.

As she replayed his words over in her head, she slowed to a prancing trot, and then paused altogether with her tail high up in the air. Sweat dripped from her body as her sides heaved with her coat partially covered in a white lather. She snaked her neck towards the ground, and at once she turned back towards Emma and took off! She broke into a canter, then to a furious gallop. *I cannot let her down,* she thought as she ran frantically back to her rider. Her sides heaved in a wicked fury as the metal stirrups continued to bang into her ribs. She thought of circling back to the barn, but her conscious kept hold of her heart. *Put my rider first. This is why I am here. I have to do this,* she thought as she made her way back to Emma.

Through the woods she saw Emma laying still and panic took hold once more. *Oh no! What if she is hurt?* Her entire body lowered towards the ground as she ripped the earth beneath her with her hooves; her eyes fixed on the young girl that appeared to lay lifeless in the tall grass.

Emma heard the sound of Ophelia's steel shoes striking the gravel road. She pushed herself away from the earth beneath her, and as she stood up she watched in disbelief as her mare came running back to her. She trembled in awe as Ophelia slowed to a trot, and then to a walk, as she approached her. The mare went right to Emma and put her head down in front of her. To her amazement, the reins were intact and still over

Ophelia's neck. Emma went towards her and cautiously reached out for them. As she did, Ophelia pressed her forehead against Emma's chest, and stood quietly as Emma sobbed. "You came back, Ophelia! You came back. Oh my God, thank you. Thank you for coming back!"

A light drizzle began to fall, cooling off Ophelia and washing Emma's tears away. Ophelia stood still as Emma put her foot in the stirrup and hopped back into the saddle. When they got back to the barn, there was no denying that something out of the ordinary had happened. Emma's breeches were covered in stains, and sweat had dried on Ophelia's neck and flanks, leaving white marks from the salt in the perspiration. Natalie took immediate notice, but chose not to say anything to the humbled girl and the exhausted horse standing in front of her. She simply turned, smiled without letting Emma see, and went outside to teach her next lesson.

Chapter 11

I Want to Go Back

Emma and Ophelia were getting along so well over the following weeks that Natalie invited the pair to enter a horse show with some of the more experienced riders from Hound Hollow. The invitation was significant to Emma, because she knew that Natalie would only invite riders to a show that they were prepared to compete in. With her newfound confidence, Emma's wounds were beginning to heal. While she was losing touch with the sweet little girl that she used to be, she was starting to open up more at home and at the barn as well.

Julia was hopeful; Chase was connecting a little more with her every day, and the therapists he was working with said that he was improving. It was not her old Chase, but Julia was grateful that they were moving in a positive direction.

Chase had also started visiting an old friend of his father's that he had looked up to growing up. Curtis was a kind, generous man that had served in the army alongside Chase's dad. After his father passed, Chase would go to him for advice, but they had lost touch in recent years. When he started therapy, one of his doctors recommended that he find someone who he could talk with that would not judge him. Curtis was that someone. He was a great listener, and he knew Chase's true personality, because he had watched him grow up. The day of the horse show, Chase went to visit with him instead of going to the competition. He wanted desperately to go watch Emma, but one of the side effects of his condition left him incredibly anxious in a crowd. When he left the house that morning, though, he made a point to wish Emma well.

"I hope the show goes well, Emma. Good luck out there."

"Thank you, Daddy," Emma replied. She tried not to sound disappointed that he was not going with them. She looked over to Julia who was holding the door open for her daughter.

"Come on honey, time to go."

Julia and Emma got in the car, and as Emma reached to put her seat belt on, she whispered quietly to her mother, "I wish he could come."

"I know, honey. You understand though, don't you? Your daddy is trying to heal, and there are some things that he is just not ready for."

Emma sighed, but nodded understandingly. Even though it hurt to see her disappointed, Julia was pleased to see the empathy that Emma had for her dad.

"Yes, I suppose I understand. I just wish he could see me ride Ophelia at our first show together."

"One day, honey. One day soon. I have faith that things are going to work out. I can already see things changing for the better."

Chase left the house shortly after Julia and Emma, and headed straight to Curtis's house. As he drove down the windy country roads, he kept noticing his mother's rosary swaying steadily side to side from his rearview mirror, like a pendulum. The swaying reminded him of his childhood when Curtis used to push him on the tire swing in the front yard of his house on his regular visits with Chase's family. This brought a smile to his face, and he began to sing a sweet hymn, not realizing the swaying cross was bringing him back to his bed time as a boy, when the cross dangled around his mother's neck as she would sing hymns to him as he fell asleep. He felt a peace in his heart that he had not felt in nearly two years, and he became flushed with a wonderful spirit and energy. So wonderful that he grinned like he had as a child as he pulled into Curtis's driveway unannounced. He found the old man outside, just finishing up mowing the lawn.

"Hey Chase. What brings you here?"

"Just looking for a chat, if you have the time."

"Sure, let me go get us some iced tea. Ruth made it this morning."

Chase sat down on the porch steps and waited for Curtis to come back. The old man sat down on the opposite side of the steps as they both looked out over the fresh cut lawn.

"Grandkids coming today?" Chase asked, taking a long sip of the tea.

"Yes, sir. They sure are. The whole lot of them! We are fixing to have a barbecue." Curtis grinned, and Chase could tell he was excited about what the day would bring.

They talked for over a half hour about his grandchildren and what they were up to, about Chase's dad, and about fishing. After a second glass of tea was poured, Curtis turned and looked at Chase with an inquisitive look.

"So, what say you? Isn't Emma's big show today?"

"Yes, sure is. They left just before I came over here."

"If you don't mind me asking, what are you doing here staring at my lawn, and drinking iced tea, when you could be watching your daughter on her horse?"

"I don't know; I just don't think I am ready."

"My guess is that if you are okay to talk about being there, you are probably okay to be there. I might not be as educated as the doctors you've been seeing, but you look and sound ready to me."

"I don't know, Curtis." Chase repeated.

"What are you afraid of?"

"I am afraid I am going to let them down. I just get so damn anxious in a large crowd. I'm afraid I might distract Emma. I know this is a big day for her, and I don't want to mess it up for her."

"You have been working so hard at this Chase. Your doctors tell you that you are ready to be in those types of situations. I think you are ready. But only you know for sure if you are. I will keep praying for you. You know it's not going to be the same for her without her daddy."

Chase looked at Curtis and smiled. His sun-darkened skin was filled with wrinkles that spoke of his wisdom, while his old, experienced eyes glimmered with a light of hope and faith.

"I'll think on it Curtis. Better yet, I will pray on it. Thank you for being there for me through all this."

"Of course, Chase. Your daddy and I were best friends. I am grateful I can be here for you."

They talked for a while longer before Chase got up to leave, and broke off the conversation by extending his hand out to Curtis. "Well, I better let you get ready for your company."

Curtis nodded in agreement with a smile.

Chase left the steps, and as he walked to his truck, Curtis put a fatherly arm around his shoulders. The old man took on a serious tone as he gave Chase one more piece of advice before Chase left.

"You got to watch the time, Chase; it just keeps going and going. But you will know when you are ready. You will feel it deep down inside, like a light that starts to shine through you. You need to find your light. It'll come back, son. Just go back to what you know best. Pray without ceasing. Love unconditionally. And as your daddy always said to you, remember to look those girls right in their eyes and tell them that you love them, *every day*. What you are going through is a struggle, there is no doubt about that, but I know you are going to get through this. Remember that you are not alone, and no one worth their salt is judging you."

Curtis's encouraging words took root in Chase's heart and he thanked him as he got back in his truck. When he returned home, he found Duke faithfully waiting for him on the porch. He took a seat next to his dog, and stroked him gently as he lay across Chase's feet. Chase put a chair cushion against the spindled porch railing and leaned back against it. He continued stroking Duke's soft fur as a light breeze cooled them both. The faint sound of the willow tree's long branches swayed back and forth in a rhythm that made a sound like the hymn that he had sung that morning in the truck, and while they listened, both Chase and his dog fell fast asleep.

Across the county at the horse show, Ophelia was even better than Emma had hoped. Ophelia worked hard for her and she jumped in fantastic form, just as she had in her lessons at home. She did not win any of her classes, but that had no effect on Emma's attitude. She was happy to just be doing what she loved, and she was so pleased that Ophelia put in such an earnest effort. Emma was slowly starting to go back to who she was just two short years prior. The time she spent with Stephen and his kind words, her mother's persistence, Ms. Natalie, and the trail ride that fateful day with Ophelia had all worked together to bring joy back to Emma's life.

As the end of the show came, everyone had gathered by the horse trailers to prepare to go home. As all the Hound Hollow riders stood talking about their rides and laughing together, a rumble of thunder in the distance hinted that a classic summer storm was about to arrive. Natalie took immediate command and put everyone into action.

"Let's go kids, get your horses on the trailer. We can finish taking care of them when we get home. We don't want to be caught in this storm."

All twelve of Natalie's riders went to work. They loaded the equipment on the trailer, tied up the hay bags, and got each horse into their stall in their respective rig. Ophelia was the last horse left to load up.

"Which trailer would you like me to put Ophelia on, Ms. Natalie?"

"You are going to go home with Cadence's mom. She is towing Cadence's mare, Melody, and she gets along well with anyone. They should get along just fine."

"Yes, Ms. Natalie," replied Emma.

The first raindrops began to fall as Emma walked Ophelia into the trailer. Emma put the ramp up behind her and then got in the car with her Mom as the rain picked up.

"We will follow you!" Emma yelled out the car window to Cadence.

"Sure thing, Emma. See you back at the barn!"

They pulled out of the show grounds slowly, and took the winding country roads back to Hound Hollow Farm. The rain started to come down harder, relentlessly pelting the windshield of the car, making it difficult for drivers to see. They came to a narrow road with wheat fields on both sides. The wheat was whipping wildly back and forth as if it were trying to warn them of impending danger. Lightning flashed often, and was close enough to light up the sky around them for several seconds at a time, casting wicked shadows on the road in front of them.

"Mommy, do you think it's okay to be driving in this? Shouldn't they pull over?"

"I don't know, honey. They should be okay. Just sit tight."

Cadence and her mother were both frightened as well, but with the barn only a few minutes away, they decided to keep going. Julia tried to stay calm for Emma as they both stared intently at the trailer in front of them making its way through the countryside.

Suddenly, Emma and Julia watched helplessly as the truck and trailer abruptly swerved right to avoid an oncoming car that had moved into their lane.

Emma screamed. "Mommy!"

The rig swerved back left, but too far.

"Mommy, no!" she shrieked in terror, looking away momentarily and gripping the door handle tightly.

The trailer cut back right, but this time, it caught the edge of the road. When it did,

Cadence's mom could not straighten it back out. Emma and Julia watched in horror as the trailer slid sideways into the ditch, and then whipped hard right, before slamming sideways into an old oak tree with the side Ophelia was in.

Julia came to a panicked stop, and before she could warn her to stay put, Emma was out of the car and running towards the wreck.

"Ophelia, Ophelia!"

Julia came running up behind Emma as Cadence and her mother got out of their truck. The mothers both grabbed their daughters to prevent them from getting any closer to the trailer; they were afraid of what they might find inside. Tears ran down Emma's face and mixed despairingly with the rain that was slowly starting to taper off.

Natalie showed up just after the accident. Once she made sure all the people were all right, she made her way inside the rig to inspect the horses. After a quick assessment, she came out and called Julia and Emma over to the side door.

"Emma, we need to get the horses out of the trailer and into another one so we can get them to the vet clinic. Once the other horses are dropped off at the farm, we will bring back one of the empty trailers to ship them."

Emma stood trembling as she listened to Natalie's instructions. First responders showed up, coloring the scene with their flashing blue and red lights, intensifying the reality of what had just occurred. Emma's voice shook as she answered Natalie.

"Yes, Ms. Natalie. But, is Ophelia okay; are the horses okay?"

"We will have to wait and see. I just need you to follow my instructions right now, okay?"

"Yes, Ms. Natalie."

Natalie repeated her directions in a calm, but urgent tone. "Now listen Emma, I need you to stay with Ophelia until we can figure out how to safely get her out and into another trailer that is drivable. Just talk to her and keep her as calm as you can. You have to *show* her how to be calm, okay?"

"Yes, Ms. Natalie, okay."

"Cadence is taking Melody out first, so I need you to stand with Ophelia. We will take her off next."

Emma and Julia climbed up to the narrow space in front of the trailer to stand with Ophelia. She was panting, and her eyes were shut halfway. There was blood running down one of her legs, but Emma could not tell how bad the injury was. Emma started to shake her head back and forth.

"I can't Momma, I can't!"

Julia grabbed a hold of her daughter. "Emma, you have to. Ophelia needs you right now."

Emma wiped her tears and sobbed. "I just wish we could go back, Momma. I want to go back!"

"What do you mean, Emma?"

"I want to start over. I want to go back to when Daddy was himself. I want to go back to when we were happy. I want to go back to when everything was simple. I am so scared, Momma."

Julia held her closely, trying to comfort her. Emma shook and continued to weep as she tried to gather the strength she needed.

Just then, they both heard the sound of a familiar truck door slamming. Moments later, the shadow of a tall man with broad shoulders took shape through the darkness and the parting rain. He came closer, making his way to the girls as they looked at him in astonishment.

"Daddy!" Emma exclaimed.

"I came as soon as I heard what happened. Honey, what can I do to help?"

"I don't know. I don't know. Just be here, Daddy. Please be here."

"Okay, Emma. I'm here. I'm here. I promise that I won't leave you."

Emma turned to Ophelia and gently stroked her forehead. She spoke to her quietly; telling her over and over that everything was going to be all right. Ophelia looked back at Emma and took a long, deep breath. Then she pressed her nuzzle tenderly against Emma's chest, and slowly closed her eyes.

Chapter 12

The Porch Swing

The next day at Hound Hollow, the breeze blew through the leaves of the sycamore trees in all directions, causing their leaves to frantically clasp together, creating sounds of uncertainty to everything around them. There was no one in the pasture to hear them though; the barn at Hound Hollow was eerily quiet.

Inside, the horses waited anxiously for Ophelia and Melody to return. There was no news though, and Doc hung his head over the stall guard and stared blankly into the aisle. Barn swallows kept flitting in and out of the barn, breaking the silence with the hyper fluttering of their wings and their shrill comments. When Natalie came out to feed, she was by herself and did not say a word to any of the horses. The horses did not clamor and fuss like they usually would at feeding time; they were all too worried about their friends who had not come back from yesterday's show. They ate quietly, and kept hoping they would hear the sound of hooves hitting the concrete aisle, but that promising sound did not come that morning.

Back at the Sterling house, Emma woke up to the sound of the porch swing creaking and birds chirping. She took a deep breath and the smell of the cornfields filled her lungs as the curtains in her room danced in the morning breeze. She shot out of bed and flew downstairs, her feet barely touching the steps on the way. She pushed the screen door open, and it slammed hard behind her against the old Victorian house. There were several robins perched on the railing of the porch that flew away in a flurry as soon as they heard the door slam shut. Emma's eyes followed them for a moment, but then looked to her left to find her father swinging back and forth on the porch swing with her mother. He was holding his wife's hand in his as the morning sun warmed both of their faces.

She stared at her parents, unsure of what to say and afraid to speak, as she was terrified of what the news could be.

"Is…is she okay?"

Julia looked tenderly up at Chase as he stood from the porch swing and walked slowly over to his daughter, leaned down and gently put his hands on her shoulders.

"Emma girl, give me your eyes."

Emma's lower lip started to tremble.

"Yes, Daddy," she quavered, locking her tear-filled blue gaze on to his.

"The veterinarian called this morning. She's going to be okay. Everything is going to be just fine, Emma. Ophelia is going to be all right."

Emma threw her arms around her father's neck and they squeezed each other tighter than they ever had before. He then twirled her around three times, before putting a dizzier, but more perfect version of Emma down in front of him.

And with that, the robins returned to the railing, their tiny feet making sounds that no one heard unless they were really paying attention. They watched closely, tilting their heads back and forth, anxious to hear what sweet Emma Sterling was going to do with her day.

"Which of all these does not know that the hand of the Lord has done this? In his hand is the life of every creature and the breath of all mankind." ~

Job 12:9-10

Acknowledgements

I would like to thank:

My wife Carice for her patience, love and support. Our life is magical because of you.

My son Kevin and daughter Kaydy. Both of you are constant sources of encouragement that make me better in all that I do.

My editor, Catherine Stone. Your talent is divine and I am so grateful that I found you.

The staff at CreateSpace. You are such an amazing team. Thank you for helping make an author's dreams come true.

My sister Vanessa for sharing your wonderful horses, Amir and Stryker.

All the wonderful, generous horses I have encountered so far in my life.

Lastly, the people that love the horse enough to listen to them, because they know deep down that the horse is always trying to tell them something that they desperately need to know.

GRATITUDE AND A
WORD ABOUT SELF-PUBLISHING

Thank you for reading *Sycamore Whispers*. I hope that the story touched you heart!
If you did enjoy my work, I would be so grateful if you spread the word to other people. When you share with people on social media, tell a friend about a book you love, and review on sites like Amazon.com, it has a *profound* effect on the success of a self-publisher like me. You really can make a difference. Thank you.

Connect with me on promotions and be the first to know about future work at www.SycamoreWhispers.com

ADDITIONAL TITLE BY AUTHOR

"Horse Gone Silent"

www.HorseGoneSilent.com

28660466R00075

Made in the USA
Middletown, DE
20 December 2018